GUNNISON'S EMPIRE

Charlie Gunnison was trouble shooter for The Cattlemen's Association. He was packed and on a train for Texas before the telegraph wires could cool. Old Man Rainsford's spread was the richest in the territory. When the word got out that he was dying, every cattle thief and land-grabber west of the continental divide would head for Skillet Range.

Gunnison knew that sooner or later the smart ones would try their luck. That's when the bullets were going to fly!

Will Cook is the author of numerous outstanding Western novels as well as historical frontier fiction. He was born in Richmond, Indiana, but was raised by an aunt and uncle in Cambridge, Illinois. He joined the U.S. cavalry at the age of sixteen but was disillusioned because horses were being eliminated through mechanization. He transferred to the U.S. Army Air Force in which he served in the South Pacific during the Second World War. Cook turned to writing in 1951 and contributed a number of outstanding short stories to *Dime Western* and other pulp magazines as well as fiction for major smooth-paper magazines such as *The Saturday Evening Post*. It was in the *Post* that his best-known novel *Comanche Captives* was serialized. It was later filmed as *Two Rode Together* (Columbia, 1961) directed by John Ford and starring James Stewart and Richard Widmark. Sometimes in his short stories Cook would introduce characters that would later be featured in novels, such as Charlie Boomhauer who first appeared in *Lawmen Die Sudden* in *Big-Book Western* in 1953 and is later to be found in *Badman's Holiday* (1958) and *The Wind River Kid* (1958). Along with his steady productivity, Cook maintained an enviable quality. His novels range widely in time and place, from the Illinois frontier of 1811 to southwest Texas in 1905, but each is peopled with credible and interesting characters whose interactions form the backbone of the narrative. Most of his novels deal with more or less traditional Western themes—range wars, reformed outlaws, cattle rustling, Indian fighting—but there are also romantic novels such as *Sabrina Kane* (1956) and exercises in historical realism such as *Elizabeth, by Name* (1958). Indeed, his fiction is known for its strong heroines. Another common feature is Cook's compassion for his characters who must be able to survive in a wild and violent land. His protagonists made mistakes, hurt people they care for, and sometimes succumb to ignoble impulses, but this all provides an added dimension to the artistry of his work.

GUNNISON'S EMPIRE

Will Cook

GUNSMOKE

First published by Robert Hale, Ltd.

This hardback edition 2003
by Chivers Press
by arrangement with
Golden West Literary Agency

ISBN 0 7540 8212 1

British Library Cataloguing in Publication Data available.

Printed and bound in Great Britain by
Bookcraft, Midsomer Norton, Somerset

1

THE HOUSE stood on a rise crowded with cottonwood trees, like a boat lifted to the crest of the biggest wave in an ocean of rolling grass. It was a two-story, wind-weathered house; large, with a porch running around all sides. The lowering sun reflected in the windows, turning them to blossoms of orange fire.

On the shady side, facing the yard and the barn and large corral and other outbuildings, two men stood smoking, saying nothing. One of them was tall, big through the shoulders and arms, and he wore an expensive pair of boots with very high heels, and a leather vest with silver ornaments and his hat was a Texas hat, very wide in the brim with a steep crown.

The man kept swinging his head, squinting his eyes and looking down the road. Finally he said, "What the hell's keeping her? She's been gone three hours." He had a deep voice and more exasperation than worry in it. His face was rather square, dark from the sun and a natural pigment; he had bold, blue eyes under thick brows, and a thin, hard mouth.

"Give it time," the other man said. Then he looked around. "What the hell, Big Sam, if she don't get back in time you're—"

"Don't say it," Big Sam Rainsford said quickly.

"Then I'll stand here and think it. That all right with you, Big Sam?"

"Do as you please," Big Sam answered.

There was about them a common darkness of hair and skin, a general similarity in the eyes that marked them as brothers, although the younger one was thirty pounds lighter. He said, "Gut-shot's a bad way to go."

"Goin' anyway's bad," Big Sam said flatly. He looked at his brother. "Where's the horse, Dal?"

"In the barn. What do you want with the horse?"

Big Sam stepped off the porch and crossed the dusty yard, the rowels of his spurs dragging, making a muted metallic noise. As he drew near the barn, he drew his pistol and held it in his hand as he pushed open the door.

The screen door behind Dal Rainsford opened and a young woman stepped out. He said, "How is he?"

"Holding his own," she said, "though I don't see how." She looked toward the barn. "Where's Big Sam going?"

"To kill the horse, I guess," Dal said. "Big Sam feels like killin' somethin', I guess."

The shot made them both jump; it sounded muffled by the barn yet it woke echoes and the door of the bunkhouse opened and two hands looked out, saw that this was none of their business and went back inside.

Big Sam came out of the barn and walked toward the porch and when he reached it, the woman said, "What good did that do?"

Dal said, "It made him feel better. Shootin' somethin' always makes Big Sam feel better."

Thumbing the spent cartridge out of his gun, Big Sam said, "One of these days, Buster—"

"One of these days what?" Dal Rainsford asked.

The woman showed a sharp irritation. "Cut it out, both of you. Why don't you go in and see him? Talk to him?" She was not a tall woman yet she was strongly put together, with good shoulders and hips and smooth arms and there was the Rainsford strength in her face; her hair was dark and her eyes were blue and she had the same firmness about the mouth, yet not hard like Big Sam's.

"I'll wait for the doc," Big Sam said. He looked again toward the road; the sun was giving out its last strong light, then he pointed. "Dust. Buggy dust. God, it's about time."

"I'll go in," the woman said. "You bring the doc in as soon—"

"I will, I will," Big Sam said. He took her arm. "Lana, he ain't got a chance and you know it."

She ripped her arm out of his grip. "That's right, but we're not holding anything away from him, do you understand? It was an accident, that's all."

Dal Rainsford turned his head and looked at her. "You ain't sorry it happened, are you, Lana?"

"I'm not glad either," she said and went into the house.

The buggy came on; there were two aboard, the doctor and a young woman; they pulled into the yard near the porch and Dal stepped down and tied the team. He started to help the young woman but she brushed his hand aside and jumped to the ground. Dust layered her clothes and sweat had made runnels down her cheeks; the doctor was getting his bags out of the back and Big Sam Rainsford was saying, ". . . No one could ever tell him anything, you know that, doc. Arabian or not, a fella in his seventies has no business on that kind of horse." He followed the doctor onto the porch. "When the horse pitched him, his six-shooter fell to the ground, went off and hit him in the belly, right here." He took the doctor by the arm and held him from going inside while he showed him where the bullet had entered.

The doctor shook himself free of Big Sam's grip, then said testily, "When they called you Big Sam, they weren't talking about your size."

"What's that mean?"

"Big Mouth Sam," the doctor said and slammed the screen door.

Big Sam looked after him a moment, then said, "Someday someone's going to hurt him." He went to the porch railing and sat down to roll a cigaret. He looked at Letty Shannon, who stood there. "Well, what's the matter with you?"

"Nothing you could help with," she said and went to the watering trough in the middle of the yard, took off her shirt and washed her face and arms.

Dal Rainsford watched her, looked at her smooth shoulders and the tightness of the shift across her back. He said, "Danged if she don't make a man think some pretty excitin' things." He looked at Big Sam and smiled. "One of these days I'll catch her in the barn and—"

"And you'll get your eyes clawed out," Big Sam said. "You don't know anything about women, Dal. Letty's not the haystack kind; she's got to invite a man."

"Well, I'm waitin'," Dal Rainsford said.

She washed out her shirt and put it on wet and it clung to her and Dal Rainsford kept watching the bounce of her breasts as she came toward the porch. When she stepped up she stopped and looked at him, looked at his sly, amused smile, then slapped him hard across the face.

He back-stepped in surprise, a hand to his cheek. Letty Shannon said, "That's for thinkin' what you were thinkin'."

"I wasn't thinkin' anythin'!" Dal protested.

"You're a liar," she said and watched him. Her hair was the color of old straw and she braided it, Indian style, letting the braids dangle. She was tall for a girl, slender, but strong, with a will that couldn't be bent or broken. This was her eighth year at the Rainsford place, the eighth year of suspicion of Dal Rainsford, for she had mistrusted him the moment she had laid eyes on him. In years she was somewhere near twenty; she didn't know exactly because Comanches had taken her when she was six or so, and held her for six or seven years; she wasn't sure how long. Old Man Rainsford had bought her for three ponies and a tin of cutplug tobacco because the Indian trouble was done with and MacKenzie's army meant trouble for any Comanche with a white prisoner and there'd been no one to claim her, no one that wanted her.

"You're kind of quick tempered," Big Sam said, smiling.

She looked at him, her eyes steady and unfriendly. "You learned your lesson once, didn't you?" She watched color come into his face, watched the scar on his cheek, the scar she had given him; he had an anger in his eyes and resentment that smouldered like a leaf-smothered fire.

"Enjoy yourself," Big Sam said. "When the old man draws his last breath, have your junk packed."

"We'll see," she said and went into the house.

The heat of the day was still thick, crowded within the walls and no breeze would come through the open windows until later, until the earth cooled. She had a room off the kitchen, a nice room with a good view of the prairie and windows that always caught the first coolness of evening.

She got a large wooden tub and placed it in the middle of the floor, then stepped out the back door to the rain barrel and brought in two buckets of sun-warmed water. She locked the door and drew the roller shade and took off her jeans; they were dusty and sweat-soaked and she put them in a corner before shedding her underclothes. The water felt good as she stood in the tub and took down her hair. Then she sponged water, letting it cascade over her head, down the firm grapefruit halves of her breasts and curved smoothness of her stomach. Her legs were long and hard-muscled and she soaped herself and rinsed, then dried with a heavy towel and put on a clean cotton dress.

While she combed and braided her hair, she listened to the small sounds of talk coming from the porch; it came through the walls, muffled and secretive, yet she recognized the voices: Big Sam's and Dal's, and it raised an anger in her because she cared more than they did and it wasn't right.

When she left her room she passed by the kitchen and supposed that she ought to start the evening meal; Sam and Dal would want to eat and she couldn't have cared less. Let them eat in the cookshack tonight.

She walked on down the hall toward the room where Old Man Rainsford was dying. As she passed the archway to the parlor, Lana Rainsford left her chair and said, "Don't go in there." She said it quick and sharp, then spoke in a softer tone. "The doctor's not through. Come sit with me, Letty."

"I don't feel much like sitting," Letty said.

Lana looked at her, then said, "Letty, I know there's no chance, you know. But I want you to stay on here. He'd wanted it that way."

"I'll leave," she said. "It's all I can do."

The door opened down the hall and she looked around as the doctor stepped out; Lana left her chair and came to the archway, her hand lifted to her throat.

The doctor brushed his mustache and said, "He wants you," pointing to Letty Shannon.

"I'm his daughter," Lana said.

"He wants her," the doctor said and opened the door for her.

She stepped inside and closed the door. The sooty shades of darkness were filling the room and a lamp on the side table spread a yellow light over the bed.

Old Man Rainsford's head turned and he smiled through the dense white mustache. "Come sit by me, girl." His gnarled hand patted the quilt, then was still. She brought a chair up and sat down and listened to the rattle of his breathing. For a moment he lay with his eyes closed and she thought he was going to go then, but he wasn't.

Within him a fountain of strength still flowed pure and strong; he opened his eyes and said, "You sent the wire?"

"Yes," she said, nodding.

"Good," the old man said, sighing. "He'll be on the train now. Tomorrow afternoon, toward evening—you watch for him, you hear. You watch for him and bring him to me. No matter who tries to stop you, you bring him to me." He put his hand out and gripped hers with a surprising strength. "You hear me?"

"Yes," she said. "How will I know him?"

"You won't mistake him," the old man said softly. "He ain't big, not like Sam. Dark hair, dark skin. Late twenties. Frowns when he's thinkin'. Don't say much and talks soft." He closed his eyes a moment as though working on a mental picture. "Like as not he'll be wearin' a pair of bat-wings with a holster sewed onto the leg. You'll know him by the way he looks at you, like he's seein' every past sin and addin' 'em up." He smiled. "They put a name to him before he was twenty-one: Charlie SixGun. You watch for him; he'll come."

"I'll watch for him," Letty said softly.

The old man remained quiet for a time, then said, "The word'll get out and in the mornin' they'll be gatherin' like flies around a carcass; Carlyle and Dannon and Burdett, they'll be here. They wouldn't want to miss my last breath after waitin' so long for it."

"The doctor will—"

"Naw now," he said gently. "He ain't goin' to do me any good. Somethin' so there's no pain, that's all. I'm too old, Letty. Time to go, that's all, but I want to go with things cared for. Of 'em all, I only trust you because you ain't got a greed. The others, they want me to die so they can cut up this ranch, cut up what I took a lifetime to build." He stopped talking and breathed heavily for several minutes. "I don't want to take away from my kin what's theirs, Letty. But I'm not going to let Dannon and Burdett have it either."

"Please rest now," she said. "You're getting tired."

"A man's got to talk while he's got the chance," Rainsford said. "You watch for Charlie SixGun, Letty. And you bring him to me the minute he gets here."

"I will," she said and got up and went out.

Lana was in the hallway, frowning. "Is he—?"

"He's holdin' his own," she said, "but I don't know how."

"The pain—?"

Letty Shannon shook her head. "The doctor gave him something." She walked on past and stepped outside to the porch. The night was almost a purple blackness and from the bunkhouse came muted talk and the clatter of tinware as the hands got ready to go to the cookshack for their meal.

The doctor stood to one side, smoking a cigar; he looked at her and said, "If he wasn't seventy—"

"He's not complaining," Letty said.

"Did he ever?" the doctor asked. "I knew his first wife and family. He was fifty when Comanches killed them all. That would have finished most men, but he married again and sired a new litter." He took his cigar out of his mouth. "I can't say that I prefer the second batch to the first."

Big Sam came out of the bunkhouse and walked toward

the cookshack and they watched him a moment. Then Letty said, "Doesn't he care at all?"

"Big Sam's had a good life," the doctor said. "He's thinking of a better." He put the cigar back in his mouth and puffed. "It's not easy to think of there not being a Skillet; this ranch was here before I came here thirty-five years ago. See those cottonwoods by the creek? The old man held court there a few times. Brought men out from town to serve on the jury when there wasn't a courtroom in eighty miles. A few men swung from those trees and every one of them got a fair trial. Yes, it's a shame to think of it going."

"It hasn't gone yet," Letty said quietly and the doctor looked at her, his manner careful, yet curious.

"Do you know something I don't know?" He took her arm and turned her so that some lamplight seeping through the lace curtains touched her face. "Didn't you send a wire while I was gathering my instruments? Something the old man wanted?"

"Something he wanted, yes," Letty said. "You going back tonight?"

"No, I'll stay until it's finished."

2

When he got off the train, Charlie Gunnison stamped his feet a few times, then walked to the end of the platform for a look at the town beyond, and the land beyond that. Behind him now were eight hundred miles of uncomfortable day coach riding and a job that might not be there when he got back and a wife who had a hard time understanding his sudden departure, yet believed his promise to send for her as soon as he could.

The train pulled out and after it had gone on, Gunnison lifted his canvas satchel and roping saddle and walked toward the main street of town. He was an angular man in a dark brown suit and a wide Texas hat and when he reached the stable, he turned in there and stood in the archway until the owner came from the back.

"I need a horse and some directions," Gunnison said softly.

The owner looked him over. "Got the horse; but I couldn't give you directions until I know where you're goin'."

"Skillet."

"Six miles due west. Can't miss it."

"I'll need a horse for a day," Gunnison said. "I'll either bring it back or have it brought back."

"Two dollars."

Gunnison paid him. "Where can a man change clothes?"

"Take any vacant stall," the man said. "I'll get your horse." He took Gunnison's saddle and went to the rear and Gunnison stepped into a nearby stall and took off his coat and tie. He put on a pair of jeans and leather chaps and got a faded canvas coat out of the satchel, then carefully folded his suit and put it away. Around the back belt of his chaps there were some cartridge loops vacant and from his satchel he took a wooden box of shells and filled the loops. He slipped an ivory-handled .44 in the holster sewed to the leg, closed his satchel and stepped out of the stall as the stable owner led a roan to the front.

Gunnison looked at the horse, walked around him once, then stepped aboard. The stable owner said, "I've never seen you before."

"That's right," Gunnison said, "you never have."

He rode out, taking the west road, a dusty slash across the face of slightly rolling prairie. This was the bigness of Texas and a man felt it as soon as he left the confines of a town, the endless sweep of the land, the unlimited horizons, and the feeling that a man could ride forever and never see the end of it.

This wasn't Gunnison's first time in Texas, yet it was not home to him. His place was the Wyoming country with the big mountains and the big rivers and the fat grazing land but he had come to Texas because the man he had met once had asked him to. He supposed that he had been born with horse-savvy; most ranch-bred boys were. And by the time he was twelve he'd learned cattle and some things out of books, but mostly cattle because that was his life. By the time he was sixteen, Charlie Gunnison was getting his man-savvy and because the country was what it was, and men were what they were, he got sixgun-savvy to round it out.

All his life he had known men who were just naturally a little better in some things than other men; better riders, better ropers, better boot makers; it was a talent, a flair these men had and they excelled without trying very hard. Gunnison found it that way with a sixshooter; he had a natural flair for it, the speed and accuracy coming easy and he figured that a man owed it to himself to parlay a talent into a living.

For some time he'd thought about it, trying to decide what to do. A lawman's life didn't hold any particular charm, and he didn't want to hire his gun to the highest pay because he wanted to enjoy his old age. He knew men and cattle, and with his talent he could always find big ranchers in too much trouble to handle and when the Wyoming Cattlemen's Association offered him a job, he took it, liked it, kept it, and earned a reputation as wide as the Sabine River in flood time.

As he rode along, he thought of the first time he had met Old Man Rainsford; he'd been representing the Association in a dispute between Rainsford, who was moving some trail-branded stock into the Territory, and one of the local cattle barons. Gunnison intended to settle the dispute, and made his decision in favor of Rainsford. It wasn't a popular decision, but it was just and he meant it to stick. The cattle baron objected, whistled, and when the gun smoke cleared, Charlie Gunnison was standing and three of the baron's "special" hands lay in the buyer's yard.

Rainsford went back to Texas and four years went by, then the telegram came; he took it from his shirt pocket and read it again:

C. Gunnison
Empire Hotel
Cheyenne, Wyoming
SHOT . . . DYING . . . PLACE READY TO GO TO HELL . . . COME AT ONCE . . . OFFER YOU CAN'T AFFORD TO TURN DOWN . . .

T. V. Rainsford

He put the paper back in his pocket and tugged his hat low over his eyes to cut the glare of the high sun. For an hour he followed the road, then he saw the Rainsford place ahead and when he reached the pole gate to the main yard, he turned in and rode toward the house.

A half dozen saddle horses were tied to the hitching rail under the cottonwoods and a knot of men stood on the porch; they all turned their heads and looked as Gunnison rode up and dismounted.

Before he could step to the porch a large man disengaged himself from the group and said, "What do you want?"

"To see Old Man Rainsford," Gunnison said. "I've been invited."

"He's dying," the man said. "I'm Big Sam, his son. Anything you can say to him you damn well can say to me."

The screen door opened and Letty Shannon stepped out. She looked at Charlie Gunnison, then said, "Will you come with me, please?"

"You get back in the house," Big Sam said and stood, his legs apart. The other men stood there with their grave, interested faces; they watched as Gunnison, who, acting as though Big Sam was not there, stepped toward the porch.

It was trouble and they knew it and there was a hush on the porch and Letty Shannon's eyes were wide and a bit fearful. When Shannon stepped within reach of Big Sam, and Sam made his move, Gunnison whipped off his hat and slashed Sam across the face with it, stinging him, blinding him for an instant. Then Gunnison hit him with his left hand, flush in the mouth, driving Sam back against the porch upright with enough force to make a few timbers creak under the impact. Sam floundered for balance and Gunnison punched his hat back into shape and stood there, waiting while Sam wiped blood from his mouth.

There was a moment when Sam thought about his gun and his hand started to move in that direction, then a thin-faced man in a flat crowned hat said, "Don't be an ass, Sam. Can't you see he's got you beat?"

"Keep out of this, Carlyle," Sam said, not glancing at him.

"I'm trying to save your life," Carlyle said dryly, "although I can't figure out why."

Letty Shannon said, "Please, there's not much time."

"Of course," Gunnison said and walked across the porch and followed her inside the house.

There were people in the hall, an elderly man with a stethoscope dangling from around his neck, and a young woman who looked steadily at Charlie Gunnison. When they drew up to these people, the doctor said, "He's holding out, mister, but I can't say for how long." He nodded toward a closed door farther down. "Go on in, but don't excite him."

Gunnison started to move past, but the young woman put out her hand. "Who are you anyway?"

"A man he sent for," Gunnison said mildly and stepped past her. Letty opened the door and he went inside; the old man looked like a wrinkled curd; his complexion was that white. But he recognized Gunnison and smiled.

"Knew you'd come," Rainsford said. "Sit. Letty, ask the others to come in here. You got paper and ink ready?"

"Yes," she said and went out.

They filed in, the doctor first, then Big Sam with his puffed mouth and the young woman; the room became crowded and they huddled against the wall as though the old man had an incurable disease and they were afraid they would catch it.

"This business of dyin' is more complicated than I thought," Rainsford said. "You write, girl. Put it all down. We'll get it signed and witnessed afterward." He looked at each of them for a moment, then went on. "This here's Charlie Gunnison, a Wyoming man high recommended to me. That's my oldest boy, Big Sam. That other fella there, that's Dalhart. Only had two sons by this wedlock. The young woman's my daughter, Lana. Letty's my ward. Same as blood kin to me."

The doctor said, "You shouldn't tire your—"

"Tire, hell! I'm headin' for a long rest." He pointed weakly to the other men. "That city-lookin' fella's Fields Carlyle. Wouldn't say he's a friend and wouldn't say he's an enemy. Ain't made up my mind about him. Never will, looks like. The others you'll know soon enough." He rested for a moment. "Big Sam, Dal, you're standin' there, waitin' for me to take my last breath so you can spend my money. Lana, I guess you got your bags all packed to go to Europe and take in the sights, but I guess you'd wait until after the funeral."

"Father!" Lana said. "What a terrible thing to say."

"When a man's dyin', he owes it to himself to be honest," Rainsford said. "Now here's what I'm goin' to do. You writin', Letty? Good. I got nearly sixty thousand dollars in cash. Each of my kin gets two thousand in cash, includin' Letty. The rest of it I'm leavin' lock, stock, and barrel to Charlie Gunnison here for a period of two years."

Big Sam groaned before he could catch himself and Lana shot him a hard look. Her mouth was grim when she looked at her father. "You don't know what you're saying, Dad."

"The hell I don't," Rainsford said. "Was I to give you the money, you wouldn't have it a year. And the land, why Dannon and Burdett there would have it away from you before you knew what happened."

The two men looked at each other, then George Dannon said, "God damn it, old man, I'm not a—"

"Ain't you?" Rainsford snapped. "Tell me you didn't start your herd on stolen beef?" He waited, breathing heavily, and Dannon fell silent. "I'm willin' everything I own to Charlie Gunnison for two years, but there's certain provisions. You gettin' this down, Letty?"

"Yes," she said and went on writing.

"A man's got to leave more than money to his kin," Rainsford said. "He's got to leave 'em ready and able to handle their affairs. Now Dal's turnin' into a card playin' boozer, and

Big Sam's goin' to end up hung if he don't stop this damned trouble-makin'. Lana, if you ever expect to get a decent man, then you got to learn how to run a home, and maybe to be a woman. Letty, I've got no complaints about at all; she's better'n the whole lot of you put together. So I'm leavin' it all to Charlie Gunnison for two years. The money that's in the bank, minus the two thousand apiece, is to be used for runnin' this place any way Charlie sees fit. In salary, he'll draw seventy dollars a month, and the banker is hereby instructed to carry these orders out." He paused to catch his breath. "Profits made in that two years are to be deposited, and at the end of that time, go free and clear to Charlie Gunnison for work done." He looked at Gunnison and found him attentive. "You've got to save my ranch from thieves like Dannon and Burdett and any others that pop out of the rocks. You've got to teach my kin how to stand straight. If they satisfy you, I hereby provide that the property and money becomes theirs, minus previously set amounts. This is my last will and testament. Doc, will you witness it after I sign it?"

"Yes," he said and stepped forward. Big Sam took him by the arm as if to hold him and Gunnison saw it.

"Don't do that," he said quietly and Big Sam dropped his hand. Letty had the document in front of Rainsford and he slowly affixed his signature, then the doctor signed it.

"You'll need another witness," Carlyle said. "May I?"

Rainsford hesitated, then nodded and Letty Shannon gave him the pen. He signed it and it was folded. "Doc," the old man said, "I want you to take this to town and give it to the judge. Charlie, you go with him to see that nothin' happens to it along the way."

"I'll do that," Gunnison said evenly.

"Now just a goddamned minute!" Dal said, moving toward the bed. He ran into Gunnison's elbow and grunted, then stood there, anger in his eyes.

The old man's voice was weak now. "Get out, except Letty. Get out."

"Do as he says," Gunnison told them and they filed out the door and moved down the hall.

George Dannon rolled his bulky shoulders and said, "There's nothin' for me here. You comin', Burdett?"

"Sure," Kyle Burdett said and they went out and mounted up.

Big Sam stood near the parlor archway; he was looking at Gunnison. "If you think you're goin' to ride in here and take over, you've got another think comin'." He pointed. "You won't last a week. I've got friends."

"Shut up, Sam," Lana said. She turned to Gunnison, her eyes frank, friendly, a smile on her full lips. "Why would a man like you come all the way from Wyoming and take a job that's nothing more than a cantankerous old man's whim?"

"I don't think it's a whim."

"We do. We'll break this in court," Dal Rainsford said. "I'm going to get what's comin' to me."

Gunnison turned his head slowly and looked at him for a moment. "That's exactly what the old man's afraid of."

The doctor and Fields Carlyle took a place near the wall; they said nothing and their presence seemed to irritate Big Sam. He said, "Let's see that so-called will, doc."

"No. You heard the old man." He put his hands in his coat pockets. "And don't try to take it away from me, Sam."

"I could," Sam said. "And he ain't goin' to get out of bed to stop me."

"He won't have to," Gunnison said mildly.

"I'm not afraid of you," Sam said flatly.

"Then do what you want to do," Gunnison advised.

He waited for Big Sam, then the door down the hall opened and Letty stepped out. "Doc, would you come—"

He left them, walking fast, and the door closed. Dal let his breath out in a long run, then said, "I'm sorry to see him go and that's the God's truth. He was a tough old bastard and I never understood him at all, but I hate to see him go."

"You goin' to cry a little?" Big Sam asked.

The door opened again and the doctor came out; he took

his stethoscope from around his neck and put it in his pocket. "Go in now if you want to. I'll send the undertaker." He glanced at Charlie Gunnison. "You ready to go?"

"Any time."

Big Sam said, "Go ahead and go. You'll play hell gettin' back."

"We'll see," Gunnison said, and put on his hat. "You wait for me, huh, Big Sam, because I'll be back."

3

Gunnison rode in the buggy with the doctor; his horse was tied on behind and they drove for nearly a mile before either spoke. "My name's Quinn," the doctor said. "We never got around to meeting each other formally." He handed the reins to Gunnison so he could pack and light his pipe. "Big Sam and the others are of the notion that Judge Caldwell's going to throw this will out. They'll be disappointed to say the least." He showed no inclination to take back the reins and hunched forward, hands idle in his lap, pipe securely locked between his teeth. "Dannon and Burdett won't figure it that way though. Not those two."

"How do they figure it?"

"Just the way it is," Quinn said. "The old man had control of his faculties until he died. The will's good, if the judge ever gets it."

"He'll get it," Gunnison said.

Quinn turned his head. "Burdett and Dannon left early."

"I saw them."

"You don't trust them?"

Gunnison said, "I don't trust anyone I don't know. Do you?"

"I find it hard sometimes," Quinn admitted.

"On the way out here," Gunnison said, "I noticed that

the road takes a long jog to the south before cutting back. Why?"

"Dannon's property," Quinn said. "He wouldn't give the county an easement."

Gunnison whoaed the team. "Take my horse and cut across Dannon's property. I'll meet you in town with the buggy."

"What—?"

"Why don't you just go ahead and do it," Gunnison suggested. "I'll meet you at the judge's house later. You wait there for me."

Quinn hesitated, then shrugged and got down and untied the horse; he grunted as he pulled himself into the saddle, then rode off toward the north and took care to stay in the swales and away from the low ridges.

Gunnison rolled a cigaret, smoked half of it, then clucked the team into motion. He wound the reins around the whip and sat there, letting the team walk along. He had gone better than a mile when he saw Dannon and Kyle Burdett squatting alongside the road in the shade of some brush.

They both stood up and Dannon held up his hand. "Where's the doc?"

"Gone to town," Gunnison said matter of factly. "He thought the ride would do him good."

The two men looked at each other, then Burdett said, "I guess you're carrying the will, huh?"

"Guess again."

Dannon said, "He didn't pass here."

"I guess he didn't," Gunnison said. He took out his tobacco and made a cigaret with his left hand; his right rested on his thigh, two inches from his .44. "I know you're not going to like this, but he cut across country where the road jogged. Under the circumstances I knew you wouldn't mind this once."

Kyle Burdett frowned. "Gunnison, why don't we go through your pockets? You could be lying to us." He stood there, his thumb hooked in his cartridge belt, watching Gunnison; then he waved his hand. "Go on, get out of here. There's nothing to be gained by this."

"That's right," Gunnison said. "It's too early to start shooting." He picked up the reins, snapped them against the horses' backs and drove on. A hundred yards down the road he glanced back and saw Burdett and Dannon mounted up and leaving.

He took a final puff on his cigaret and shied it away and drove on, thinking about these two men, both big men with land and a good payroll and each dreaming of being a lot bigger; they were not like Big Sam who acted and thought about it later. These men were planners and they hadn't started trouble along the road because it would have gained them nothing. They were, Gunnison thought, dangerous because they never let their emotions stampede them into foolishness.

Gunnison didn't hurry and arrived in town late in the afternoon. As he drove down the main street he saw a man cleaning the walk in front of the general store and he stopped and asked directions to the judge's house, then drove on, turning onto a side street and going three blocks to a gabled house surrounded by a neat fence.

The stable horse was tied up at the hitching post and Gunnison got down and walked toward the porch. The door opened and an elderly man in a frock coat said, "Come in. We've been expecting you." He offered his hand. "Judge Caldwell. You're Gunnison?"

"Is the doctor here?"

"Come and gone," the judge said. He led the way to the study. "I'm sorry to see the old man go; he was a fixture in this part of the country. Even those that didn't like him respected him." He offered Gunnison a chair and a cigar, which he took. When he had it going, the judge said, "I looked over the will. Perfectly legal. I sent a boy down to see if he could find Harry Wilson at the bank." He took out his watch and looked at it. "He ought to show up pretty soon, unless he's out of town. But I don't think so." Caldwell frowned and scratched his nose. "Funny I never heard the old man speak of you, Mr. Gunnison. You've got your work cut out for you. No one's ever been able to handle Big Sam and

Dal. The girl's headstrong too. But then I expect you're the same way."

"You left out Letty," Gunnison said.

Caldwell shrugged. "Who counts Letty? She's no real kin. If I was her I'd take the two thousand and light out. Get a new start somewhere else. She was Indian took as a child and likely served a buck; they took 'em young, you know and—"

"I know about Indians," Gunnison said. "The old man left her a fourth of the place and I'll see that she gets it. Have you got a sheriff in this town?"

"No," Caldwell said. "The county seat's in Buckley, twenty-six miles west of here. I'm home because court isn't in session, otherwise I'd be—" He looked at Gunnison, then said, "No, we don't have a sheriff. He pays a part-time deputy though. Hank Freeman. Tends bar over in Sintown."

"Where's that?"

Caldwell said, "You come in on the train? Must have. As you rode down the main drag, did you notice—no, I guess you didn't. You keep ridin' on through town and you'll come to it. About twenty years ago old man Rainsford made up his mind that the town wouldn't do much growin' as long as the saloons and the gambling and the ladies of the night walked the streets, so he ran them all out, made them put all their sin in one place you might say. People started calling it Sintown. They don't come here and—well, I wish I could say we didn't go there. Too many do, I'm afraid. Payday nights the main street is nearly vacant, except for a few in the stores. All the money goes to Sintown." He shook his head. "The old man had other reasons to regret it. Big Sam and Dal hang out there all the time. They're pretty big in Sintown."

"I'll have to look into it," Gunnison said mildly. "I'm not against a little sin now and then."

"They'll know you," Caldwell said. "But you do what you want."

"I thought I would. What kind of a game do Burdett and Dannon play?"

"Rough," Caldwell said, "but they don't play together."

Gunnison showed his surprise. "Not friends?"

"Good enemies," Caldwell said. "They've been crowding each other off and on now for years. I suppose now that the old man's gone—" He took his cigar out of his mouth. "So that's what the doctor was talking about; you met them on the road. No trouble?"

"It's too early," Gunnison said. "They'll let Big Sam do something stupid and see how it turns out." He got up. "Straight down the main drag you say?"

"My advice is not to go there," Caldwell said, rising. He offered his hand. "Good luck. Call on me—"

"I will," Gunnison said. "And tell the banker I'll drop in on the way out of town." He put on his hat and went outside to his horse and swung up. Cutting back to the main street, he had a look, then turned and rode to the end of it. Vacant lots separated Sintown from the rest; it was built in a line on the prairie, split by a very wide street and the judge had been right, the business was there, for the hitching racks were jammed with tied mounts. Gunnison rode the length of the street, reading the names of the saloons: THE PRAIRIE BELLE, CATTLEMAN'S REST, POKER ANN'S, THE BEST PLACE. There were no stores, not even a decent place to eat, for the saloons gave free lunch with their drinks. Gunnison saw a few places with the shades drawn, and there were two places devoted to gambling of all kinds, and that was about the extent of Sintown, except for the three dozen shacks that served as homes for the ones who never left this lively place.

Gunnison stopped a man crossing the street and asked him where he could find Hank Freeman and the man pointed to The Best Place and Gunnison swung around and found a place to tie up. He moved through the crowd of idlers outside and walked across the dirty sawdust to the bar. A few heads turned toward him but they didn't make a point of looking, although he knew that nearly everyone in the room knew he was there, and that they hadn't seen him before.

He bought a beer, took a drink of it, then said, "You Hank Freeman?"

"That's my name." He was tall and slender and he wore a pearl-handled pistol in a cross draw holster. "I don't know yours."

"Charlie Gunnison." Heads on either side turned and listened. "Where can we talk?"

"Here," Freeman said, smiling; he had a bold, handsome face and a full mustache with a natural lift to the ends.

"I thought somewhere a little more private—"

"I'm among friends," Freeman said. He worked the bar rag in a loose circle, wiping up nothing. "Talk or forget it. You're wastin' my time."

Gunnison sighed and put both hands on the bar. "Tell you what I'll do—we'll have a little shoot out." Freeman's eyes widened, but there was no fear in the man and Gunnison knew that he had guessed right; the pearl-handled pistol wasn't an ornament. The men at the bar fell quiet and Gunnison spoke softly. "You set up a couple of shot glasses and we'll both back away twenty feet or so. At a signal, we'll draw and fire. If I bust my glass first, you and I'll talk where it's private. If you beat me, we'll do it your way."

"If you want to shoot so bad," Freeman said, "why don't you just face me and move when you're ready?"

"That would be pretty foolish," Gunnison said. "One of us is bound to be better and my way you or I will live to practice a little." He smiled. "It'll make the last time more interesting."

A man down the bar said, "He's got a point there, Hank. If he's anywhere near as good as you, it'll be some contest."

Freeman shrugged. "What the hell, I'm not against somethin' new." He placed two shot glasses on the bar, three feet apart, then came around to the customer's side. Men backed away to give them room and the crowd outside drifted in because the tenor of noise was being hushed and this meant something.

Freeman bounced on the balls of his feet. "How do we work this?"

Gunnison pointed to the man who had spoken up. "Let him give the signal."

"When I say: go," the man said and waited, his jaws working on his chewing tobacco. "GO!"

Gunnison didn't give Freeman a thought, didn't give him a consideration as to his speed or accuracy; he concentrated on what he was doing, drawing smooth and fast, letting the hammer drop as the muzzle leveled. The shot glass vanished and he rolled his thumb across the hammer again, shattering Freeman's glass a split second before the deputy's bullet gouged into the splinters.

Then he looked at Freeman, who stared, then said, "That just can't be!"

"Did you get a late start?" Gunnison asked.

"Hell, no, I didn't," Freeman said. He looked at his gun, then holstered it and grinned. "Where would you like to go to talk, mister?"

"Got a back room?"

"I'll bring you a fresh beer," Freeman said and went behind the bar.

Gunnison reloaded his .44 and dropped it into the holster, then walked to the bar; men made an elbow free alley for him and the talk started to pick up. Freeman had two beer steins and he nodded toward the back.

After he closed the door and perched on a beer keg and drank some of his beer, he said, "If I'd had my way I'd be dead, wouldn't I?"

"Likely," Gunnison said. "But you were too smart for that." He sat down and rolled a cigaret. "Old Man Rainsford is dead. I'm running his place now."

"Big Sam won't stand for that."

"I'm running it," Gunnison said again; he looked steadily at Hank Freeman. "I've got complete control of Skillet range and wealth for two years. If I asked for the law, what would I get?"

"Me," Freeman said.

"Tell me just what that means."

"I go by the book, Gunnison. No favorites. Never have

been." He grinned lopsidedly. "Until three minutes ago I had the kind of a pistol that could make it stick. Now my reputation is some tarnished."

"You can polish it," Gunnison said. "Are you afraid of Burdett or Dannon?"

"No," Freeman said. "Why?"

"If they lean on me, I'll fight," Gunnison said. "But I'd rather swear out a warrant if I knew it would be served."

"I get eighteen dollars a month for this job," Freeman said. "That's not much, but I've never took a dime when anyone's back was turned or failed to do my duty. If I didn't, friend, no one would, because no one wants the job. And I mean no one."

Gunnison smiled and drank most of his beer, then put the glass aside. "I expect you'll be practicing, huh?"

Hank Freeman shook his head and smiled. "I'm a first-rate talent in a small town and I'm happy with it. But both Burdett and Dannon have money and they can hire some *real* two-pistol talent. You know what I mean? I didn't know you from anyplace, and the name doesn't bring to mind any reputation I ever heard of. You're better than me by far, but then maybe I'm not really very good at all." He sighed and finished his beer then wiped the foam off his mustache. "Maybe I'd better practice at that. It could be that we'll have to stand side by side again against some important talent, and I wouldn't want to disgrace myself." He laughed at the humor of this, but Gunnison knew how serious was the thinking behind Freeman's remark.

It was as he suspected and as Freeman had confirmed; both the cattlemen would hire their fighting and they had the money to pay for the best.

4

The rain came before dawn and it lasted an hour, then blew away and the sun came out and steam rose from the ground. Gunnison left the hotel and walked to the stable to get his horse, saddled, and left town, taking the road to Old Man Rainsford's place. He was in no particular hurry, yet he maintained a steady pace and overhauled three buggies in a two mile span. They were, he supposed, friends of the old man going to pay their last respects.

When he passed under the pole arch he saw the horses and buggies crowded into the yard, and the large knot of people on the porch. He saw Big Sam near the barn; he was mounted and he had five Skillet riders with him. When he saw Gunnison he wheeled his horse, whooped once, and dashed across the yard. People stopped talking and turned their heads and Big Sam drew his gun and bent low over the horse's neck.

Without hesitation, Gunnison took his rope from the saddle, made his loop and started whirling it open as he spurred to meet Big Sam. They rode directly toward each other, then as they drew near, Big Sam raised his gun and triggered a shot as Gunnison disappeared over the side of the horse.

A cry rose from the people on the porch because it looked like Big Sam's shot had counted, then Gunnison made his cast from under the neck of the running horse and he caught the two front feet of Sam's pony, snubbing him down; Big Sam sailed through the air, arms and legs thrashing, his yell going up long and strong before he hit and bounced and hit again to lay still.

Gunnison freed his rope from the thrashing horse and it got up and shook itself and trotted to the barn; Gunnison rode on, coiling his rope and the Skillet riders watched him but did not try to stop him.

He dismounted and tied up by the porch, then he saw Letty Shannon standing there; she was looking past him and he followed her glance. Three men were trying to get Big Sam to sit up and they were having trouble because he kept falling over.

Letty Shannon said, "A man could hurt himself in a fall like that." The way she said it, as though it didn't matter, told him that she didn't like Big Sam, and he wondered if she liked any of the others.

The people on the porch watched Charlie Gunnison because he was a stranger and because he'd just done violence to a man and it didn't matter to them that Big Sam had started it; they knew Big Sam and could keep out of his way.

Letty Shannon took him by the arm. "Come on in the house. You don't want to go to the funeral, do you?" Gunnison shook his head and followed her inside. They went into the parlor and Lana Rainsford turned from the window.

"You've hurt Sam." Then she looked past Gunnison; the preacher was standing in the hall, looking grave and full of sympathy.

"We're ready now," he said solemnly. Then he turned his marble-cold eyes on Gunnison. "There was no need to profane this day with violence."

"Tell that to Sam," Gunnison said dryly. "Or didn't you see him take a shot at me?"

"A man in his grief—"

Letty Shannon interrupted him. "They're waiting for you, Reverend."

He glared at her. "Evil will come to this house," he said, then stalked out.

Lana Rainsford pulled a dark veil over her face and stepped to the hallway. Letty said, "Is that to hide your tears or the fact that you have none."

"After all he did for you," Lana said, "the least you could do is to stand by his graveside."

"He knows where I stand," Letty said. "He always knew."

They waited in the parlor while Rainsford's family and friends moved to the clump of trees on the knoll; the ceremony was held there and in the silence they could hear the rumble of the preacher's voice casting out the devil; the words were indistinct, but the tone was clear. After the coffin was lowered and the grave covered, everyone came back to the shady portion of the yard and the Mexican cooks began to serve the food, and the mood changed; there was talk and laughter and some of the men got a little drunk.

Dal Rainsford crossed the yard and came in; he stopped at the archway and looked at Charlie Gunnison. "Big Sam said he could stop you. I didn't think he could." He took off his hat and started to step into the room, but stopped when Gunnison spoke.

"Tell the foreman and the old man's family I want to see them in half an hour. We'll use the old man's office."

"It's locked," Dal said. "We can't find the key."

"Because he gave it to me," Letty said.

Dal clapped his hat back on his head. "I'll see what I can do," he said and went out.

Taking the key from Letty, Gunnison walked down the hall and went into Rainsford's office. It was full of orderly clutter, old saddles and hanging ropes and mementoes of his many years of violent living.

The books were in the desk and Gunnison went through them; it was a picture to him, of hirings and firings, good years and bad, profits made and lost, and troubles encountered and overcome. From these figures Gunnison could see the change from open range to the windmill and barbed wire, the change from the Texas longhorn to shorthorn Herefords and entries for freight bills marked the coming of the railroad.

Someone started to open the door, then thought better of it and knocked before stepping inside. He was a big man with a dense mustache, in his middle forties, with enough cruelty in his eyes to make a good foreman.

"I'm Gator," the man said. "I run this spread."

"You run it for me," Gunnison said evenly. "Sit down." He watched the man a moment. "Let's have all of your name."

"The rest is French; you couldn't pronounce it anyway. They call me Gator because my folks were Cajun, the Bayou country." He took out his tobacco and made a cigaret. "I saw you handle Big Sam. Good rope work." He smiled. "The other day I thought that maybe a gun was about all you could handle."

There was a heavy step in the hall, then Big Sam limped

into the room; Dal had his arm and helped ease him into a chair. Sam looked at the scarred toes of his boots until Gunnison said, "You made a damned fool of yourself, Sam. Don't do it again."

"I damned near broke my back," Sam said sullenly.

"You could have died out there," Gunnison reminded him. "Try to keep it in mind that I'm only so tolerant." He looked up as Letty and Lana stepped in. "Close the door, please." He turned the swivel chair around and looked at them. "I don't see any red eyes, but then I didn't expect any, so you'll understand if I get down to business." He let his glance touch Dal and Sam. "What do you two do around here anyway?"

"Do?" Sam asked. "Why, we work our—"

"Don't lie to me!" Gunnison snapped, tipping forward in his chair. "You booze it up and play cards in Sintown!" He looked at Gator. "Are you a liar or what?"

"Now wait a min—"

"Then you answer me straight out: what do these two do around here?"

"As little as possible," Gator said.

"You just lost your job," Big Sam said angrily.

"He's lost nothing," Gunnison said. "Gator, put these two in the bunkhouse with the other hands and work 'em. Forty a month."

"All right, but there'll be trouble. They've shot their mouth off and the crew'll make it hell—"

"You put your money down and take what you buy," Gunnison said.

Lana Rainsford said, "You just love to lord it over people, don't you?"

"I've just looked over the books," Gunnison said, "and I've got enough trouble without having a couple of half-grown kids on my hands. Gator, how long has this rustling been going on?"

"What rustlin'?" Sam asked.

"Shut up and let him answer," Lana said.

The foreman shrugged. "A year, maybe a little more. Nothing big you understand. Calves mostly. A few now and then, like cats had been at it, if there was a lot of cats, which they ain't."

"Fences cut?"

Gator shook his head. "Never found any, not even a cut and a splice. It worried the old man."

"I guess it did," Gunnison said. He looked at each of them. "The old man loved you and he let you have your own way. Well I don't love you and you won't get your own way with me." He put his hand on the payroll book. "We've got ten men. Dal and Sam makes two more. Put four on fence riding right away and along the section bordering Dannon and Burdett. See that they're carrying repeating rifles."

Gator nodded and got up. "That's all?"

"For now," Gunnison said. "Take your two hands with you."

Dal helped his brother up, then said, "You won't last, Gunnison." They went out and Lana stood there as though she dared him to tell her what to do.

Gunnison stared at her, then said, "You're a proud woman, aren't you?"

"All the Rainsfords are proud," she said.

"Not all of them." He continued to look at her. "Can't you wait two more years?"

"Why do I have to? I could take my two thousand and leave now."

"Why don't you?" He smiled. "Or couldn't you stand the thought of Letty and the others splitting your share?"

"I'll outlast you," she snapped and walked out.

Gunnison sighed and motioned for Letty Shannon to sit down. He pulled paper and pen to him and wrote for ten minutes, then sealed the letter in an envelope. "When you go to town, I want you to mail this. It's to my wife. I want her to come here and live."

"I . . . didn't know you were married."

"How could you know?" He gave her the letter. "She's expecting late this fall. If she doesn't travel now, she won't be able to."

"I'll mail the letter," she said, getting up. At the door she paused. "Gator is a strange man. He's holding back his judgment of you."

"Why, I expect him to," Gunnison said.

"And Dal and Sam won't do what you told them."

He smiled. "And I expected that. But we'll see."

After she left, he told two of the servants to move a cot into the office; he would make it his sleeping room. They carried the horsehair sofa out and brought blankets and a wash stand and his satchel.

It was his intention to eat his meals alone, but he thought better of it and had supper that night in the dining room, at the big table; he sat at the head of it, and since Dal and Sam were having cookshack fare, there was just Letty because Lana would not leave her room.

And when the servant started to take her a tray, Gunnison made him take it back.

He was drinking his coffee when Gator came into the house; he stood there, looking amused. "Dal and Sam left twenty minutes ago."

"To ride fence?"

"They went to town," Gator said.

"You gave them permission?"

He shook his head. "I told them to ride fence."

"Thank you," Gunnison said. "Have a horse saddled and brought to the porch." He finished his coffee and got up and went to his room and came back with his gun and a holster; he buckled this on, tied the thong around his leg and shrugged into his coat.

Letty Shannon watched him, then said, "They'll be expecting you, Charlie."

"Then it wouldn't be right for me to disappoint them, would it?"

He went outside to wait and as he stood on the porch he saw most of the crew by the bunkhouse, watching him, and he knew why, and knew they'd be there when he got back. Gator brought up a leggy roan with fire in the eyes and the round muscles of a runner; Gunnison went into the saddle quickly and the horse pitched twice before he checked him and wheeled out of the yard.

Lana came out of the house and looked after him, then said, "Where's he going?"

"After your brothers," Letty said.

"How lucky does he think he is?" She looked at Gator and at his slight amusement. "You think this is funny?"

"I guess I do," Gator said frankly. "I don't have much use for a man who can't look in another man's eyes and know when to mind." He wiped a gnarled hand across his mouth, brushing his dense mustache. "Can't none of you folks see that he ain't foolin' around?"

He wheeled and walked across the yard and Lana looked after him. "I never liked that man."

"What did you ever like?" Letty asked and waited for her answer.

"I'll like it when you're gone."

"Don't hold your breath."

"You're not wanted. You never were," Lana said. "What right do you have to take a man's goodness and cut yourself in for a share?"

"I never asked for anything and I've been grateful for what I got," Letty said. "Do you know what's the matter, Lana? You're not getting what you want. Your father was old and you thought you could wait until he died then have things your way. But he brought Charlie here and he's just like your father, only younger, and maybe tougher and you're not going to be able to wait now. You'll have to do for him what you never did for your father. You'll have to be a woman instead of a willful kid."

"I ought to slap your face!"

"You won't," Letty said evenly, "because you know I'd knock half your teeth out if you tried. Don't bully me, Lana. I've never taken it."

"You're happy, aren't you? Gunnison's your kind, isn't he?" She laughed disdainfully. "You'll be in his bed before the week's out."

"Would that make you unhappy, Lana?" Letty asked. "He wouldn't have you on a bet, you know."

She stood there a moment, glaring at Letty, then whirled and went inside and slammed the door. Letty remained on the porch, watching the sun reach down to touch the edge of the earth. It would be dark by the time Gunnison got to Sintown, dark and full of trouble for him. But she supposed he was not bothered by it because that was what he liked, the smell of trouble; it was in his eyes and the restless way he moved and in the tone of his voice when he spoke to men.

It's not my place to worry, she thought, and went into the house.

5

Sintown was noisy and bright with lamplight when Gunnison tied up in front of The Best Place saloon and he walked up and down the street, stopping to look into windows. He stepped into Poker Ann's for a moment, had his look and moved on to the Prairie Belle. He really didn't expect to find them, but men would notice him and pass the word along. He checked the Cattleman's Rest, then walked back to The Best Place and went in.

Hank Freeman was tending bar, his deputy's star brightly polished; he smiled and waved as Gunnison stepped up to the bar, then he came down, a stein of beer in his hand. He shoved it toward Gunnison and said, "Some of the boys mentioned that you were looking over the town."

"Now why don't you tell me where they are?" Gunnison said. "I'm supposed to find out."

Freeman shook his head. "Damn it, I hate to see you get hurt, Charlie, and that's what it's heading for."

"I've been dared," Gunnison said. "What would you do?"

"Think it over carefully," Freeman said. He looked at

Gunnison and sighed. "All right, they're at Poker Ann's place."

"I didn't see them."

"They're upstairs in Ann's room. And there's about fifteen toughs downstairs waiting for you to try to get up the stairs."

"I see."

Hank Freeman started to take off his apron. "I'll go along."

"You stay here," Gunnison told him. "It's no good if I get help. Dal and Big Sam are a couple of bad little kids; they've got to be spanked." He winked and walked out of the place and down the street.

There was no traffic in or out of Poker Ann's place and Gunnison stopped and looked inside. Ten men stood at the bar, all watching the door, and another five sat at a table near the stair and he knew that Freeman was right; he'd never make it up the stairs.

Carefully circling the building, Gunnison looked it over and found a way to the roof; he saw that he could go around near the eaves to the front and he supposed the lighted windows near the rear of the building marked Poker Ann's rooms; he could see the windows from the alley and the edge of roof that ran by them.

Returning to the main street, he walked back to the other part of town where everything was quiet and found the hardware merchant closing up for the night. The man unlocked his store again and Gunnison made his purchases, had them sacked, then walked back to Sintown and went into an alley.

Sitting down on the edge of a horse trough, he opened the sack and took out a stick of dynamite, a cap and a piece of fuse. He slit the stick, inserted everything carefully, then packed a ball of mud around it. Walking down the alley a bit, Gunnison climbed on a rain barrel and onto a low porch. It was just a step from that roof to Poker Ann's and he made his way around to the front porch overhang. Squatting there, he struck a match, lit the fuse, and watched it sputter, then made a down cast and flung the stick under the porch just inside the front door.

Quickly he moved around the side to the back and Ann's window and he heard an alarmed yell go up, then the explosion and the frame building shook and glass splintered; he raised his foot and kicked in the window and with an arm over his face, flung himself through.

He hit and rolled and came up, .44 in his hand. Poker Ann was by the door, about to open it, and she froze there, a slender, pale woman with large eyes and a thin, humorless mouth. Dal Rainsford was on the bed; he jumped up, but stopped there and waited. Big Sam had been playing solitaire at a table near the center of the room; he made no move to get up.

"You boys played hookey," Gunnison said, getting up. "Let's go."

"What was that explosion?" Dal asked.

"I threw a stick of dynamite in the front door," Gunnison said.

"You wrecked my place," Poker Ann said and ran out. She got to the top of the stair and saw the damage and wailed loudly.

Gunnison wiggled the muzzle of his pistol. "Let's move."

Dal Rainsford picked up his hat and clapped it on his head, his expression sulky. Big Sam said, "Damned if I'm goin'. No man's goin' to run me."

There was no hesitation in Gunnison; he stepped close to Big Sam and wiped the barrel of his gun across his head and as he slumped, Gunnison grabbed him and hauled him out of the chair. He dragged him to the open door and said, "Move, Dal. I won't tell you again." He motioned with the gun. "Down the stairs."

Dal Rainsford started down and Gunnison dragged Big Sam to the edge, then booted him with his foot and sent him rolling, bouncing down and he caught Dal halfway, caught him behind the knees and upset him; they thrashed to the bottom together.

Poker Ann's place was empty; even the bartender was

gone. She stood in the center of the room looking at the wreckage. The dynamite had cleaned out the front of her place, wall and glass, throwing splinters inside and across the walk. There was a crowd in the street and Poker Ann said, "Who's goin' to pay for my place?"

"Charge it to your friends," Gunnison said. "Lift your brother, Dal."

"He's pretty heavy."

Gunnison frowned. "Do I have to tell you everything twice?"

The effort wrung a grunt from him, but Dal Rainsford got his brother to his shoulder and staggered outside with him. Their horses were tied down the street and Gunnison walked him down there, then helped Dal get Big Sam across the saddle. He tied him hand and foot and Dal stood there and watched, then said, "Won't someone give me a gun?"

A man, anonymous in the crowd, said, "You don't want a gun, sonny."

Whirling, Dal tried to single him out, to take out his anger on this man, but Gunnison touched him on the shoulder. "Mount up."

The words hardly fell when Dal Rainsford whirled, meaning to catch Gunnison off guard, but he didn't; he swung around, aiming his fist and Gunnison cracked him across the crown of his hat with the gun barrel and caught him with his free hand as he fell. He holstered his pistol and boosted Dal across the saddle, and tied him there, then led the two horses down the street.

The crowd made way for him and then Gunnison saw Hank Freeman standing to one side, a sawed-off shotgun in the crook of his arm. "I had a notion you'd do it somehow," Freeman said, "but I just had to see how." He nodded toward Ann's place. "A stick of dynamite sure raises hell, don't it?"

Gunnison said nothing; he went on, leading the horses, then he untied his own and stepped into the saddle and turned out of Sintown. As he crossed the vacant lots separating the two towns, he saw men standing quietly on the boardwalks; the hardware merchant was there, hands in his pockets and as Gunnison passed, he said, "If I'd known what you wanted the dynamite for, mister, I'd have given it to you."

"You've got more dynamite," Gunnison said. "And there's Sintown. Go blow it up if you want."

"It's not my fight," the merchant said.

"Whose is it then?" Gunnison asked. He heard Big Sam groan and he stopped and got down and walked to a nearby watering trough and brought back a hatful of water; he dumped it over Sam's head.

"Untie me," Sam said.

"You had your chance to sit straight," Gunnison said and mounted his horse.

The merchant said, "That must be mighty uncomfortable, ridin' that way."

"Ask him when you see him again," Gunnison said and rode out of town. He moved along briskly, now and then trotting the horse and Dal and Sam began to yell at the punishment, then they stopped that, needing all their strength to keep from having the wind jolted out of them.

Gunnison raised the lights of the Rainsford place and walked his horse for a mile, but when he passed under the pole arch he went the rest of the way at a gallop, wheeling near the bunkhouse and flinging off. The hands were still there and Gator came forward; he motioned for some men to help him and they picked Sam and Dal off their horses and carried them inside.

Lana came out of the house and ran across the yard and saw what was going on. Gunnison said, "Gator, I told you what to do with those men. You do it."

"Are they—" Lana started to say, then whirled to Gunnison. "You hurt them, didn't you? You just had to hurt them."

"Go back in the house," Gunnison said and turned his back on her. She hit him with her fist, once on the neck and once on the shoulder and he paid no attention to her at all and this set her to crying; she wheeled and ran back to the house.

Gator watched her go, then said, "What makes you run, mister?"

"I don't like all the things I do," Charlie Gunnison said. "But I do 'em anyway, because someone has to. The old man spent twenty-five years spoilin' his kids. I've got two years to change all that."

"I never thought of it that way," Gator said.

"Maybe that's why the old man didn't ask you to do the job," Charlie Gunnison said and went into the house. He had one of the servants bring a tub and some water so he could bathe and while he was finishing dressing, a knock gently shook his door.

"Come in." He looked around as Letty Shannon stepped inside. "What do you want, Letty?"

"I'm going to town in the morning. Is there anything you want me to get for you?"

"Some work clothes," he said and fished in his pocket for a twenty dollar gold piece and handed it to her.

She closed her hand around it and said, "I tried not to worry about you tonight, but it was hard not to."

It touched him that she would think about him, and it worried him because he didn't want her thinking about him. He said, "Letty, after I leave, what happens to you?"

"I don't know."

"Will you stay?"

She shrugged. "I'm not his blood kin, but if I left, where would I go? What good would two thousand dollars be to me? Nothing can touch me here, but anywhere else I'd just be another woman who's been taken for a squaw."

"That was a long time ago, Letty."

"I know it, but people remember those things."

"Some don't," he said gently. "Go to bed, Letty."

She hesitated, then went out, softly closing the door and he blew out the lamp and stretched out on his cot. The house was quiet, but it was an uneasy silence, a silence full of disturbances and it was a time before he went to sleep. The first flush of dawn woke him and he got up, dressed, and went to the table for his breakfast. He ate quickly and went outside; Gator was giving the crew orders and Gunnison walked across the yard.

Dal and Sam were there, carrying themselves stiffly, but when it came time to mount up, they got into their saddles and left with the rest of the fence crew. When Gator had put them all to work, Gunnison said, "Catch up a horse and ride with me."

The man nodded and went to the corral; he brought back two and they rode out together. When they came to the gate an hour later, Gator said, "That's Burdett's land over there."

"I know that," Gunnison said and unlocked it, swung it wide and they passed through. He refastened it and they rode on for two miles then topped a small rise and saw the house and outbuildings backed against a creek.

As they came into the yard, two men stepped from the barn and walked toward them. One of them, a raw-boned man wearing a battered hat said, "Now, I know him—" he nodded toward Gator, "but I don't know you." The front door opened and closed and Kyle Burdett came out and teetered on the edge of his porch. The man said, "Mr. Burdett, is it all right if I find out these fellas' business?"

"You do what you want to do, Jonas," Burdett said and smoked his cigar.

The man with Jonas stepped over and faced Gator. He said, "I ain't goin' to have trouble with you, am I?"

Gunnison said, "I'll take care of this, Gator. Behave yourself."

Jonas smiled pleasantly. "That's sensible." Then he glanced at the holster sewn to the leg of Gunnison's chaps. "That's a funny place to carry a gun. You don't mind if I laugh?"

"Enjoy yourself," Gunnison said. "Just don't make a mistake."

Jonas pulled his mouth into an O of mock surprise. "What would that be? Suppose I put my hand on my own pistol? What then?"

"I'd have to figure you were goin' to use it."

"Well, mister, when I touch my pistol I *do* use it. Now

you've got no business on this here land. I'm goin' to teach you not to come back."

He waited, then his hand smacked as he slapped the butt of his gun and he got very little farther than that; Gunnison wiped the .44 out of the holster, rolled off his shot and sent Jonas spinning with a broken shoulder. The unfired pistol flew out of Jonas' hand and plopped in the dust and he rolled once after he hit, then lay there, thrashing dust with his feet.

The man watching Gator forgot all about the foreman; he stared at Jonas, then at Gunnison and said, "Jasus now."

"Help him," Gunnison said and turned to the porch. "Burdett, you could have stopped that. Why didn't you?"

"Jonas likes to learn for himself." Then he shrugged and took the cigar out of his mouth and his dark eyes mirrored his disappointment. "And I thought he could do the job. My mistake."

"Don't make too many of them," Gunnison advised. "Are you alone?"

"My wife's inside. My two boys are out tomcattin' around somewhere. Why?"

"I like to say my piece just once," Gunnison said. "Burdett, I wouldn't go easy on any man who stole from Skillet."

"Are you accusin' me of stealin'?"

"No. I'm telling you not to."

Burdett drew on his cigar. "You can't hold all that range together, Gunnison. It's too big for one man."

"You may be right, but before I lost it, there'd be people hurt. You might be one of them." He stepped back and walked to his horse and swung up.

From the porch, Burdett said, "There are a lot of men faster than you, Gunnison. All a man has to do is send out the word and pay regular."

"Is that what you're going to do?"

"Already have," Burdett said evenly. "And when I get my crew together, we'll ride on Skillet and take it."

There was no sense in talking further, Gunnison saw; Burdett had his mind set on expansion and he was tough enough to push it, and had the money to pay for any help he needed. Gunnison turned away from the porch and stepped to his horse. Jonas was on the ground and his friend had taken his shirt off and was trying to stop the bleeding; a group of Burdett riders stood by the barn, not wanting to mix into this.

Gunnison said, "Let's go, Gator." He swung up, pulled his horse around, still looking at Jonas. Then he moved near and said, "I'm sorry," and rode out, cutting across Brudett's land to the Dannon place.

6

Henry Stiles knew he was a good dry farmer and in the second year on his place he broke even and turned a small profit on the third. His neighbor didn't make it but he was a stubborn man and hung on until the end and Stiles bought his place, even though Skillet's fence cut into it like a wedge of pie.

Stiles was a man afoot and he had a natural distrust for the man on horseback and that far flung corner of Skillet fence always bothered him. He watched it carefully so that no strands remained broken long; he didn't want Skillet cattle on his land, not because he was selfish with grass, but because he knew the Rainsfords would make trouble over it.

Once a week Stiles would straddle his mule and ride out to the west pasture and look at the fence and his wife always worried on that day and he wished that, after thirty-one years of marriage, a woman ought to stop worrying.

As Stiles approached the fence he saw the broken strands, then he saw the calf in his pasture and the critter's ma on the other side, kicking up a fuss. He swore and tried to chase the calf back through the tear in the fence but the critter acted frisky and the mule was stupid and a little clumsy and after twenty minutes of this Stiles decided he'd have to get a rope on the calf somehow and drag him back.

His work with a rope was limited to tying a load on a wagon and he wasted another twenty minutes before he managed to get the rope around the calf's hind foot. He dragged him bawling and kicking toward the tear in the fence, sweating and swearing to himself, and he was on Skillet land and trying to urge the calf to join him when he stopped and looked at the two men sitting their horses not thirty yards away.

Big Sam said, "What are you doin' with the calf, farmer?"

"He's yours and I'm tryin' to get him back," Stiles said.

"He's ours all right," Dal Rainsford said. "You know us?"

Stiles swallowed hard. "I seen you in town a couple of times. The old man's boys, ain't you?"

"That's right," Sam said. "We own that calf."

"Then take the damned thing," Stiles said. "And string some new wire along here. I'm tired of fixin' it."

"We've just your word you ain't been cuttin' it," Dal said.

"Now see here—!" Stiles stopped, not wanting to lose his temper. "The old man knows me. He knows I wouldn't cut a fence."

"The old man's dead and buried," Sam said. "And we don't know anything like that at all."

Stiles remained silent for a moment. "I'm sorry to hear he's gone. I always got along with him." He handed the rope to Sam, but he wouldn't take it. "Well, here," Stiles said, "take your calf."

Sam shook his head. "It looks to me like you was stealin' some beef."

"That's a lie! Any damned fool could see I was pullin' the calf onto your property."

"It didn't look that way to me," Sam said.

"Let it go," Dal Rainsford said. "Let's fix the fence and—"

"I've just been called a damned fool," Sam said. "Farmer, you've got yourself into some trouble. Rustlin's a serious—"

"Rustlin'?" Stiles angrily whipped off his hat and flung it on the ground. "Damn you, Sam Rainsford—"

"Don't cuss me!" Sam warned.

"Then don't accuse me of stealin'!"

"Let him go," Dal said gently. "Why make anything of it?"

"Because people are always makin' somethin' of it with me," Sam said. "Now you drop that rope and put your hands in the air, farmer. Dal, see if he's got a gun."

"I ain't got a gun," Stiles said, angry now. "And I ain't puttin' my hands in the air." He made a sudden fling with his arm, intending to throw the rope to them and Sam Rainsford pulled his gun. He shot from the hip and Stiles clapped a hand to his breast and tried to hold onto the mule's mane with the other; he continued to stare at Big Sam for a moment, then he slid off his mule and fell in the grass.

Dal said, "Why the hell did you do that?"

"A man can take just so much of a pushin'," Sam said, "then he's got to push back."

"You just ain't gonna leave him lay there, are you?"

Sam holstered his gun and shook his head. "I'll stay here. You go to town and bring the deputy back with you. Stiles was stealin' a calf; that's the story and we're goin' to stick to it."

"What the hell else can we do?" Dal said. "Aw, Sam, damn you anyway!" He wheeled his horse and rode out and Big Sam watched him go, then got down and turned Stiles over with his foot.

The man was dead and Sam wished that Stiles had been carrying a gun; a gun would make things a lot more convincing to Hank Freeman. He hunkered down and smoked several cigarets; it would be hours before Dal got back and Sam began to regret his burst of impulsive violence.

He wasn't sorry he'd killed Stiles. He was sorry he hadn't done it more cleverly.

His horse snorted and he looked up, stood and looked around. In the distance he saw two riders on the crest of a rise, looking his way; they started to move toward him and Sam Rainsford felt a moment of panic; he wondered if he should mount up and light out.

Then he realized that it wasn't any good because he recognized the two men as riders for George Dannon, and if he could recognize them, they certainly knew who he was. They came on across Stiles' land and through the break in the fence.

One of them bent in the saddle to look at Stiles. "Dead, ain't he?" His glance touched his partner, then Big Sam. "You shoot him?"

"He was rustlin' a calf," Big Sam said.

"So," the man said. "Look that way to you, Slick?"

"It could be," Slick said. "He try to shoot it out, Sam?" He swung down and walked around. "Where's his gun, Sam?"

"I thought he had one. Turned out he didn't. But he reached like he had a gun."

"Then I hope you got witnesses," Slick said. "I knew a guy who got hanged because the other fella didn't have a gun."

"There's no need for talk like that," Sam said. "Dal was here. He rode into town for the deputy."

"One brother testifyin' for another don't sound too good," Slick said. "Now if the farmer had a gun—"

"I sure wish he did," Sam said wistfully.

Slick looked at his friend and winked. "Tell you what, Sam. I'll ask Roddy here if he'll let you have his gun. Just as a favor. How about that, Roddy? You want to leave your gun there on the ground by Stiles?"

"I don't know," the man said. "I don't want to get mixed up in this, Slick."

"Now you're not goin' to get mixed up in anything," Slick said. "Why don't you do Sam a favor?"

Roddy scratched his beard stubble. "Well, Sam's never been big on doin' anythin' for me. Now that's a fact, Slick, and you know it."

"Well, maybe he will after this," Slick said. "How about it, Sam? You'd appreciate this, wouldn't you?"

"I sure would," Sam said. "Come on, Roddy. I always thought you was a good sort."

"How good?" Roddy asked.

"Just what do you want?" Sam asked. He looked from one

man to the other. "Just what you two doin' over on Stiles' land anyway?"

"Lookin' for a break in the fence," Slick said. "We thought we'd steal two or three calves." He grinned and took out his smoking tobacco. "Roddy and I've been doin' that for some time. Make a little extra that way. Dannon gives us five dollars apiece for the calves. Now if Roddy leaves his gun, you'd have to overlook that, Sam. You understand?"

"A few calves don't make that much difference to me," Big Sam said. "Let's have the gun."

"Go ahead, Roddy," Slick said. "Give him your gun."

Roddy handed it over and Sam stood with it in his hand, as though he were not quite sure what to do with it.

Slick said, "You ought to put it in Stiles' hand, Sam. Make it look like he was drawin' on you."

"I guess I'll just throw it on the ground beside him."

"Put it in his hand," Slick said. "That way Roddy and I can be a witness in case you ever go back on your deal."

"Now, I wouldn't do—"

"Hell," Slick said. "Sam, I know you. Put it in his hand."

When they were half a mile away from Fields Carlyle's place, Gunnison could see that Carlyle was in the horse business; the man's barn was surrounded by neat corrals and breaking pens and as the two men rode into the yard, Carlyle climbed down off a corral fence and met them by the pump.

"I wondered if you'd pay a visit," Carlyle said and offered his hand. He was tall and dressed in gray riding pants and he wore a white shirt open at the throat and tufts of dark hair curled there. "Come on to the house. I have some cold beer in the cistern."

Gunnison and Gator remained on the shaded porch while Carlyle went in; they watched the activity at the corral where a dozen wranglers worked horses. Gator said, "Carlyle breeds good stock."

The man came out with heavy glasses wearing a foamy collar. He perched on the porch railing and smiled. "From the dust on your clothes and the sweat on your horses, I'd say that you've been visiting today. You saw Dannon and Burdett?"

"Yes," Gunnison said. "You might say that I'm lining up the targets in case anyone moves against Skillet."

"And you want to include me?" Carlyle asked.

"It depends on you," Gunnison said frankly.

Carlyle shrugged and sipped his beer. "I have a thousand acres here, Gunnison. Bought and paid for. Ten years ago I knew I couldn't raise cattle because I wasn't big enough to push Old Man Rainsford off his property, not any of it. I love horses, fine horses, so I mortgaged and bought breeding stock from Kentucky. Now I raise the finest coach horses in north Texas. I sell to the stage lines—or what's left of them—and to the army and to people who like to drive a good team. A small portion of my business is selling saddle stock, and in the last three years I've been bringing in ponies from Utah for work horses." He leaned forward and tapped Gunnison on the kneecap. "To tell the truth, I wouldn't raise cattle. I make a good profit off my thousand acres and don't want any more."

"I'm in the market for a good horse," Gunnison said. "What can you show me?"

"Come along," Fields Carlyle said, and they took their beer and walked across the yard to a corral behind the barn. The horses were in a large pasture and Carlyle said, "Take your pick."

Gunnison looked them over carefully, then said, "That roan looks good. Cut him out."

Carlyle whistled and a rider came into the pasture through a side gate and shook a loop into his rope. "The big roan," Carlyle said, and they stood there while the rider made his cast and led the roan over to the fence where Gunnison waited. Climbing over, Charlie Gunnison looked the horse over carefully, then nodded.

"He's magnificent, isn't he?" Carlyle said. "Two hundred dollars, and that's not a bad price."

Gunnison looked at the roan for a moment, then dug

into his watch pocket and counted out ten twenty dollar gold pieces and gave them to Carlyle. "Pokey," Carlyle said, "put his saddle on the roan and lead rope on his other horse. Gunnison, if you'll come to the house I'll give you a bill of sale."

Again they sat on the porch and Carlyle went in; when he came out he gave Gunnison a bill of sale, which he put in his pocket. "I could have given you the horse," Carlyle said, "or charged you half that price, but I'm not buying any favors. I earn my own, and I pay my own way. Dannon and Burdett want to split Skillet range between them, then they'll start fighting among themselves until one has it all. I want no part of that."

"How can you stay out of it?" Gunnison asked. "They may decide your place is worth having."

"Except for one thing," Carlyle said softly. "Neither outfit can whip me." He nodded toward the men working in the corrals. "This place is more than a horse ranch, Gunnison. It's a haven for men who have no place to go, men who've shot themselves quite a reputation in other parts of the country and want to live quietly where no one will bother them. I carry sixteen men on the payroll all year 'round. Ten of them are top ranking gunfighters. But I have rules, Gunnison. Rule one: a man can't be wanted for so much as spitting on the sidewalk in Texas and work for me. Rule two: there are no sidearms worn on this ranch except on Saturday afternoon, for pistol practice. Rule three: there is no fighting allowed except on Saturday morning between ten and twelve; all quarrels are settled there on the grass in front of everyone."

Gunnison looked at him for a moment, then laughed. "I'll be damned."

"Is it funny?" Carlyle asked seriously. "These men are tired of one town after another. They like it here."

"And who keeps the rules?"

"I do," Carlyle said modestly. "I'm thirty-four, Gunnison. When I was twenty I was known as the Wind River Kid." He raised his hand to his lean face and dense mustache. "I've aged, but in Montana and the Dakotas they'd still recognize me, I'm sure."

"The Kid had a big pistol reputation," Gunnison said. "I've heard of you." He made a wry face. "I don't blame Dannon and Burdett for leaving you alone. Could you be telling me to do the same?"

"Not at all," Carlyle said. "Gunnison, we have no quarrel with Skillet. None at all. We have none with anyone unless they go out of their way to make one with us."

"There'll be trouble between Skillet and the other two brands," Gunnison said softly. "Carlyle, can we count you on our side?"

"No. We want to stand clear of it."

"Can you?"

"Well, we can try," Carlyle said and finished his beer. He smiled. "Why don't you ride over on a Saturday afternoon? Pony Deal's here, and Joel McKitrich and some of the others. They'd enjoy shooting with you."

Gunnison got up and shook his head. "I don't shoot for fun."

"What man does?" Carlyle said seriously. "Tomorrow's a hill a man just can't see over until he gets there. Maybe you'll change your mind. We're all friends here."

7

Hank Freeman knelt and studied the dead man; Big Sam and his brother stood to one side, and Freeman took a notebook from his hip pocket and wrote a few things down, like the time he arrived and the way the body was stretched out and the break in the fence. Finally he got it all down for his report to the sheriff, and stood up; he had taken the gun from Stiles' hand and he looked at Dal Rainsford.

"You didn't say anything to me about him being armed."

Dal looked at his brother and didn't understand how the

gun had got there, but he couldn't say anything about it. He licked his lips before speaking. "Hell, a man gets rattled over a thing like this, Hank. What do you expect?"

"You get rattled over a shootin'?" Freeman looked at him a moment, then shook his head. "Somehow it just don't set with me." He pushed his derby to the back of his head and wrinkled his brow. "Stiles drew on you? Now why in hell would he do a stupid thing like that? He was just a dirt farmer."

"I guess he knew what kind of trouble he was in, stealin' the calf," Big Sam said. "All I know is that he reached and I did the same and got my shot off first."

"Yeah, so you said," Freeman murmured. He raised his glance to a far rise and saw the two horsemen there, then watched them come his way. Finally he recognized Gunnison and Skillet's foreman, and Sam and Dal looked at each other and shuffled their feet in the grass.

When Gunnison rode up he dismounted without a word; he walked around the dead man, looked at the ground, then stood there, his lips pursed, looking displeased. He saw Stiles' hob-nailed boots and his bib overalls and Gunnison knew the truth; it was in his eyes when he looked at Big Sam. "He drew on you first, I suppose?"

"He sure did," Big Sam said.

"How was he carryin' his gun?"

"In his hip pocket, I guess," Big Sam said.

Gunnison pointed. "He stuffed a .45 with a seven-inch barrel into his hip pocket? You're a liar, Sam. You pulled down on him cold."

"That ain't so," Sam said and swallowed hard.

Gunnison continued to stare at him and finally Sam dropped his eyes to the toes of his boots and kept them there. "Well he's dead," Gunnison said quietly. "The harm's done. Where does he live?"

Hank Freeman pointed. "About a mile or a little less. Got a wife and a daughter. The boys have gone their own way. Charlie, do you want me to—"

"He was killed on Skillet range by a Skillet man," Gunnison said. "I'll take him home and tell his wife." He turned and looked at Sam and Dal. "Unfasten your gunbelts and let them drop."

They looked up and Dal said, "What?"

"I won't tell you that again," Gunnison said and waited and they defied him for a moment, then both reached for their belt buckles and let their weapons drop. "I don't want to see either of you carrying a gun again. Do you understand that?" His glance touched Sam. "I can't prove anything, can I? You'd lie and your brother would swear to it. Now go on, get out of here and do your work. I'll take care of you when this thing settles down." He stepped up to his horse and got his rope and with Hank Freeman's help they tied Stiles across his mule and passed through the break in the fence.

They didn't travel far before they saw Stiles' place and as they drew near the low shanty, his wife came out, saw him draped across his mule and screamed. She ran to him and got in the way when they tried to lift him down. Finally, Freeman took her bodily away. The girl stood just outside the door, her dark eyes round and full of tears as Freeman laid the dead man on the ground.

"Ladies," he said. "Please—go on inside now."

The girl started to obey him but the old woman jerked away. "No!" she shouted and stood there, her face contorted in helpless rage. "You just bring him home dead and that's all there is to it? You just bring him home and put him on the ground and we're supposed to go on livin'?" Her finger stabbed at Hank Freeman. "You're the law around here. Ain't you got anythin' to say?"

"There was a quarrel over a calf," Freeman said. "Your husband had his rope on a Skillet calf. There was an argument and he pulled his gun."

"He wasn't carryin' a gun," the girl said.

"What kind of gun?" the woman asked.

"A pistol," Gunnison told her. "A long-barreled .45 pistol."

"He never owned such a gun," the woman said. She closed

her eyes and wrung her hands. "What'll we do now? You tell me what we'll do?" She looked from one to the other. "How come you ain't arrested nobody?"

"There were witnesses who swear your husband pulled a gun," Freeman said.

"They're lyin'! Who shot him?"

Freeman looked at Gunnison, who said, "Big Sam Rainsford."

"Ah," the woman said, as though this satisfied her, answered her questions completely. "The old man's gone; everything's changed. My Henry lived in peace with the old man and we were both fools enough to think it would stay that way." Her glance settled on Charlie Gunnison. "Who are you?"

He told her. "I'm running Skillet now."

"This way?" She pointed to her dead husband.

"We'd be pleased to bury him for you—" Gunnison began, but she cut him off with a quick wave of her hand.

"I don't want you to touch him! Get off my land!"

He knew there was nothing to say. He had seen this before, women crying when their men were brought home, and in a way it was the way of cattle country when farmers came in; every intention to keep the peace sooner or later was broken by gunfire and it was the farmer who paid dearly for it.

Catching up his horse, Gunnison stepped into the saddle and in that way forced Freeman to do the same; they wheeled and rode out and when they were away from the yard, Freeman said, "There ought to have been something you could have said to her, Charlie."

"There was nothing to say. And nothing to do, Hank." He dropped the reins and rolled a cigaret as he rode along. "It's a bad thing, and in the long run, it'll go against us. There was a time when there was more of our kind than there were Stiles'. But that's changed. God damn Sam anyway. This will turn public opinion against Skillet."

"Where did Stiles get the gun?" Freeman asked.

"You tell me," Gunnison suggested. He looked at Freeman

and the deputy was troubled about this; his mouth was drawn into a tight line and he kept squinting his eyes.

"Dal came to town and left Sam alone there at the fence," Freeman said, then he veered away. "Let's go back."

It suited Gunnison and they rode back to the break in the fence and dismounted and walked around carefully, examining the tracks, sorting them out. Freeman pointed and said, "You can see where the calf came through—right out there on Stiles' property. It's plain to see that he chased the critter considerable before he caught it."

They sorted through a jumble of tracks and could make out where Stiles had brought the calf onto Skillet land; Freeman was across the fence but Gunnison was examining the ground on Stiles' side.

"Come here a minute, Hank." He stood there and Freeman came over and Gunnison pointed. "Two riders; the tracks are plain enough. Gone off in that direction. Dannon's place is not far from here; as I recall his fence line is no more than a mile at the most."

Freeman had his look at the tracks, riding out a way and then riding back; he crossed the fence and looked at the fresh tracks there, then came back. "I guess I know where Stiles got the gun." He took off his derby and scratched his head. "I don't understand it though. None of Dannon's men are friendly with Big Sam."

"Things change," Gunnison said. "I don't know as we can do anymore, Hank."

"That seems a damned shame," Freeman said. He looked carefully at Gunnison. "You adding up somethin' in your mind?"

"If I get an answer I'll let you know." He waved and rode on, crossing over onto Skillet range and in an hour raised the ranch house and outbuildings; he rode to the barn and dismounted there and Gator came out. Gunnison swung down and Gator whistled a man over to take the horse away, then Gunnison said, "Big Sam and Dal get back on the job?"

"Yep."

"I meant that about their carryin' guns."

"I know it. They won't. Anyway, not where they think you can see it."

"I want six men tonight with shovels," Gunnison said. "Tell them to form quietly by the barn after dark. I'll join you there."

Gator nodded, but asked no questions and Gunnison knew it would be that way, for Gator knew how to work for a man, how to do his job and yet maintain himself as his own man. A cattleman called this loyalty to a brand, but it was more, it was a way of living, of having confidence and showing it and Gunnison was flattered by it. A crew pretty much followed a foreman, and as long as Gator stayed in line, Gunnison had little to worry about.

There was no one at home except the servants. The Mexican housekeeper told him that both the women had gone into town earlier in the day and weren't expected back until after dark. Gunnison went to his room and stretched out on the bed and slept until the cook's triangle woke him. He ate, watched the sunset, then when it got dark he went to the barn and found Gator and the men waiting.

Gunnison said, "I want every man carrying a rifle. Gator, send someone to the cook and get some cold meat and biscuits." A man broke away to take care of this and Gunnison had horses brought up. The man came back from the cookshack carrying two flour sacks and they all mounted up and rode out of the yard.

He led them back to the break in the fence and they dismounted there; he spoke to Gator. "I want three shallow trenches dug on this side of the fence and three on the other. Keep them far apart, yet close enough to where rifle fire will cover the opening in the fence. The horses can be picketed over there someplace." He waved his hand toward the south. "Along about dark every night I want men belly down in the trenches. And I want the dirt they dig up scattered around so's someone riding near here in the daytime won't see what we've done."

"We waiting for something special?" Gator asked.

"I think Skillet is ripe to lose some stock," Gunnison said. He said it matter of factly, without raising his voice and they all heard it and looked at each other, but made no comment.

Gator placed the men where he wanted them and started them to digging and in an hour he went around with Gunnison and made his inspection. The trenches were nearly three hundred yards apart, with the break in the fence halfway between them.

Gunnison said, "It's my guess they'll come through here, and tonight. I want them to pass through, cut out what calves they mean to steal, then catch them on Skillet land. I'll fire the first shot. Pass that around."

"We've been waitin' for a night like this," Gator said and trotted away.

He sat down on the ground after Gator left and let the night cover him and he felt the cool wind on his face and breathed the flavors of earth and grass and decided that it was a shame that man had to spoil it. And man always did because man always wanted more than he needed. Man with his inbred discontents and greeds and his penchant for violence when denied.

By occupation, Charlie Gunnison had come to know these men well; he understood their ruthlessness because he had a ruthlessness of his own. Their greed was no secret to him, for his ambitions were real and driving, a force constantly push-him on. There never was a time in his life when he handled the trouble of other men because he felt any humanitarian impulse to right the wrongs of the world; he worked for a fee because he wanted land of his own and a life of his own and a year ago he thought he had it, a nice place and a wife and a fair-sized herd, but then anthrax fever hit and by the time a vet was brought in, Gunnison had lost too many to make his place pay.

He was faced with selling out or mortgaging heavily. Neither appealed to him. Then Old Man Rainsford's wire came and there was the answer; let the land fallow and go back to it when this job was done, this one last final job; he'd have money in his pocket, more money than he needed.

He knew why he was sitting in the dark, waiting, because he knew men like Dannon and Burdett; they were bold men who would move fast; he was that way himself and by knowing himself he also knew the men he fought; they were alike and Gunnison supposed that they could be friends, under other circumstances. He had known times when he had worked for the big ranchers and drove homesteaders out and when he had worked for homesteaders and pushed back the big cattlemen and because of this he actually saw no clear cut sides to a fight, no line of who was right and who was wrong; a man fought for himself no matter how he covered it up with fine phrases or noble causes.

He would fight Dannon and Burdett because they were standing in his way of doing a job, standing in the way of his profit. Gator would never understand that because he worked for pay and loyalty to the brand while Gunnison was a maverick with no brand at all.

The foreman came back and hunkered down beside Gunnison and sat that way for a time, not saying anything.

Finally Gator said, "We goin' to spend the night here?"

"If we have to," Gunnison said.

"How can you be sure they'll come through here?"

"Because I would if I was rustlin' from Skillet." He looked at Gator, the shadow of him squatting there. "If I hadn't come here there wouldn't be any fight between Dannon and Skillet. Big Sam and Dal wouldn't put up much of a scrap. And when the boss runs, the hands don't stay long. Not even you, Gator. But Dannon knows me. He knew me right off. So did Carlyle and Burdett. It makes it more interesting for them. That's why they'll lose no time picking our herd. They want to show me it can be done."

"I never would have figured it like that," Gator said.

"You're not in my business," Gunnison said.

He fell silent then and they waited for over two hours before any sound came to them save the wind in the grass. Then he heard horsemen approaching the fence and he and Gator got up and faded back. There was a faint night light, and stars, but no moon at all and he made them out, six men stopping at the break in the fence to have a low-pitched conversation.

Then they came through, in single file, and rode onto Skillet land and out of sight. Yet they were not so far away that they couldn't be heard as they worked the cattle around and cut out twenty head.

There was some loud swearing and a "Ya! Ya!" as they tried to work fast, then they had what they wanted bunched up and started driving them toward the break in the fence, and Gunnison let them come on, let them get halfway through before he broke the night silence with a gunshot.

8

He fired his shot high, not intending to hit anyone because he knew that Gator and the other Skillet riders would not be so generous, and he was right, for in the first volley of rifle fire one man yelled and threw up his hands and was lost in the dust and milling cattle.

For some twenty seconds it was sound and fury and wheeling horses and rank confusion, then the rustlers broke and ran, leaving a dead man behind, and the shooting died off a gun at a time. Gator was yelling for someone to bring up the horses and Gunnison stood up, in no hurry now. Three of the Skillet men were hazing the cattle back away from the fence, then the man came up with the horses and Gator mounted and led Gunnison's horse over.

He said, "I didn't expect 'em to break and run."

"What else could they do?" Gunnison said. "We cut loose and they couldn't tell whether we had ten men or thirty." He swung up. "Have the break in the fence fixed, but hurry it up. I want to ride."

"On Dannon?"

"Who else?"

"I'll fix the damned fence myself," Gator said and dismounted. "Hurry it up there!" he yelled. "Come on through!" He waited until the riders came through the break, then pulled and twisted the wire in place and hurriedly mounted up.

Someone said, "I know the dead man, Gator. He rides for Burdett."

"That's right," another said. "And I saw a fella called Slick. He rides for Dannon."

Gator said, "I guess that's all we need, Mr. Gunnison."

"It's all I need," Gunnison said. "We'll hit Dannon's first. I want those men, but if I can't have them, I want to shake Dannon up good and proper." He looked at the men sitting their horses near him. "Is that understood."

They murmured and nodded and they were feeling pretty good because the boss had been right and they liked working for a man who could come up with a good guess.

"Then let's not sit around here," Gunnison said, and led the way out. He set a fast pace but had no notion of catching anyone; they would be wearing out their horses getting to the bunkhouse and fixing up a story. Not for a moment did Gunnison believe that this had happened without Dannon's knowledge and permission and he wondered what would be the best way to take care of this.

He thought about it hard and finally when they raised the lights of Dannon's place he pulled up and the Skillet riders gathered around him. "Gator, we'll all dismount some distance from the place and go in afoot. Pick two men and have them sneak into the corral and spot the lathered horses." He pointed to a long-bodied young man. "You come with me. We'll circle the house and come in through the back if we can. Gator, I want you to get around in behind the bunkhouse and when you hear the commotion, throw down on Dannon's men and keep them out of action. You other four cover the yard. There'll be no shooting unless I start it. Understand?"

They murmured that they did and rode on a bit farther, then swung down and tied their horses in a small grove of trees. The two men who were going to the corral left first and Gunnison gave them ten minutes, then he motioned to Gator and they split up, each circling the yard and buildings for a different destination. Gunnison noticed the silence with which the young man moved and he spoke softly. "What's your name, boy?"

"Shag."

"Stick close to me."

"Try and lose me," Shag said and grinned, his teeth making a light slash across the darkness of his face.

They moved carefully around the house; the lights made yellow squares of the windows, but there was no sign of movement. There was considerable litter in the yard and they picked their way along, not wanting to stumble on anything and make a noise. Gunnison and Shag moved close to the wall, close to a partially open window and raised up to look inside.

They could see a man on the sofa in the parlor; a woman had her back to them and then she dipped a cloth into a pan of water and they could see that it was bloody. Then George Dannon came in view; he had a repeating rifle cradled in his arm and he looked at the man, then said, "No sound of anything, Cora. Is it bad?"

"His shoulder's broken," the woman said. "You should get a doctor, George."

"All right, all right! He'll do 'til dawn, won't he?"

Gunnison pulled Shag close and whispered in his ear, then gave him a shove and the young man ran quickly around to the front of the house. When his boots thumped on the porch, Dannon whirled with the rifle and it was then that Gunnison poked his .44 through the window and said, "Put it down or you're a dead man."

Dannon froze for a moment, then slowly lowered the rifle to the floor and Gunnison could see his face, see the surprise and anger there. Shag opened the front door and covered them all with his rifle.

"Hold 'em there, Shag," Gunnison said.

"They ain't goin' no place," Shag said and Gunnison went

around the house. On the porch he yelled: "Bring 'em all out here, Gator!" He went on inside the house and kicked Dannon's rifle into a far corner.

George Dannon said, "You've got the damnedest luck I ever saw."

"No," Gunnison told him. "You have. You're still alive." He went over to the sofa and looked at the man there, young and hurt, and the woman, who was Dannon's wife; she watched him with fear in her eyes. "We'll get you to town, mister," Gunnison told him. "I don't want you bleeding all over the sheriff's jail."

There was a growing hubbub of sound out in the yard. Gunnison motioned toward the door. "Get on out there, Dannon. Shag, find a couple of lanterns." He prodded Dannon to the porch and saw that Gator and the others had rounded up the crew and had disarmed them.

"They're missing a couple," Gator said. "One they left at the fence and one more. Found two horses lathered up."

"Have a buckboard hitched up," Gunnison said. "And fetch a rope."

"What for?" Dannon said. "What the hell is this?"

"I'm going to show you what happens when a man rustles Skillet stock," Gunnison said. One of his men tossed him a rope and he wove a hangman's knot in it while they all watched him. Then he tossed it over a porch beam and let it dangle.

Shag came out with two bright lanterns and hung them so that the light spread to the men standing by the porch; they watched the hangman's rope and then George Dannon said, "God damn it now, you can't hang a man!"

"What would you do if you caught a man rustling your beef?" Gunnison asked flatly and looked at Dannon, waited for the only answer the man could give.

Dannon swallowed, and his wife, standing in the doorway, made a small strangling sound in her throat, then put her hand over her mouth. "Well, I've never hung a man," Dannon said finally. "Ain't we goin' to get a trial?"

For a full minute, Charlie Gunnison let the silence run

strained and deep, then he said, "Gator, get the wounded man in the buckboard. Pick a man to take him to town. We've got a call to make." Then he looked hard at Dannon and pointed to the rope dangling from the porch beam. "Mister, I don't know how fast you learn, but if you make one more move against Skillet, I'll hang you where I find you."

He waved his hand then and Gator got the prisoner into the buckboard and sent a man away with him; the others waited for Gunnison. "Get your horses and bring them up," he said. "We'll wait here with Mr. Dannon." They moved away and Dannon's wife let out a long sigh of relief; Gunnison glanced at her and she turned and went into the house.

Dannon relaxed a bit and let his breathing go deep and regular. "I knew you'd come when Randy came back, but I thought I could handle it." He put his hand to his vest pocket and brought out a cigar. "Have you ever hung a man, Gunnison?"

"Yes."

This surprised Dannon, to hear him admit it. He said, "Then I guess I came closer than I thought."

"You came damned close," Gunnison said softly. "Watch yourself."

Dannon nodded and lit his cigar. "You're a professional. I can't quite get the idea through my head. You do just what you have to do, whether you like it or not. Me, I do something because I want something. It don't make sense to me, you fightin' to hold the old man's place. After you're gone I'll take it away from Big Sam and Dal anyway."

"You may not even be around," Gunnison said, and stepped off the porch; Gator rode up with his horse and he mounted, then held his gun on George Dannon while Shag stepped into the saddle.

"You forgot your rope," Dannon said bravely.

"No, that's for you," Gunnison told him and rode out, his men trailing close behind him. They reached the road and swung left and followed it for three miles where it forked and there was a sign there on a leaning pole, a board with a star burned into it with a branding iron; one end of the board was pointed to indicate direction.

Gator said, "Burdett will be waiting too, boss."

"I expect he will," Gunnison said. "So let's not keep him."

"We're just goin' to ride in?"

"We'll look it over first," Gunnison said and pushed on.

They finally came to a gate and Gator opened it and they passed through and rode on to Burdett's ranch house; it was dark, but there was a light in the cookshack and Gunnison didn't slacken his pace. But when they rode into the yard he motioned for them to fan out.

The cook came out with a lantern, holding it high over his head. He saw the brand on the horses and said, "They're in town, waitin'."

"You the only one here?" Gunnison asked.

"His wife and kids is in the house," the cook said. "You want them?"

"No."

"Didn't think you did," the cook said. "He said to tell you he'd be waitin' at Poker Ann's, if you wanted him bad enough."

"How many men are with him?"

"Three. They'd been doin' some ridin' earlier tonight and kind of needed a change of climate." He squinted at Gunnison and smiled. "The other boys, well, they've all taken a sudden likin' to fence ridin'. Couldn't wait 'til mornin' to get at it. Beats all, don't it."

"I have no quarrel with them," Gunnison said. He looked at Gator and phrased his question carefully. "Aside from yourself, who's good with a gun and reliable in a fight?"

"I guess Shag's your man," Gator said. "I'll go too."

"One's enough," Gunnison said, and to protect the man's pride and reputation, added, "I want to save you for the big one, Gator."

"You're the boss," the man said.

"Take the boys back before they wear out the night," Gunnison said. "Shag and I'll go on into Sintown." He pulled his horse around and rode out of the yard and as they passed through the gate, Shag sided him and they rode that way, holding an easy pace, in no hurry and yet not loafing along.

Gunnison was not surprised that Burdett had gone to town; he would feel more secure there among the bright lights and traffic and he likely had friends there he could count on. It figured because there was a touch of the big-mouth in Burdett; he liked to have people notice him and an audience would be welcome when it came to a fight because his reputation depended on people talking it up..

When they reached town Gunnison did not ride right on through the avenue of closed and darkened shops; he stopped in front of a feed and implement store and dismounted. There were no horses tied; the street was completely vacant and silent except for the strident sounds coming from the brightness of Sintown three blocks beyond.

After tying up, Gunnison lifted his .44 from the holster, punched out a spent cartridge and replaced it, along with another under the normally empty chamber. Shag saw this and said, "Six beans in the wheel tonight?"

"They put six holes in it, didn't they?"

He chuckled and lifted his rifle off the saddle horn where it hung by a thong and ring. It was a .44-40 Marlin with the barrel and magazine tube cut off to twelve inches. He filled the magazine, levered a live round into the chamber and let the hammer carefully down to half cock, then pushed another shell into the magazine.

"What does that hold, bob-tailed like that?" Gunnison asked.

"Seven now," Shag said. "You ready?"

"Nothin' holdin' us back," Gunnison said.

"We just goin' to walk in on 'em?"

"It's the best way. Shag, if it goes to pieces, don't hesitate. You understand?"

"I'm wound up like a ten-day clock," Shag admitted.

They walked side by side down the street, past the buildings, past the vacant lot separating the factions of the town, then they angled across the street toward Poker Ann's place. The front of the building was cross-hatched with hastily-erected planks to cover the windows and the smashed door frame.

Shag said, "What the hell hit that? The Dallas Express?"

"Stick of dynamite."

"Aw, come on."

"A stick of dynamite," Gunnison repeated.

They made the boardwalk and looked in through the cracks in the planks and studied the interior of the saloon. For a moment Gunnison failed to find Burdett, then Shag tapped him on the shoulder and pointed.

Kyle Burdett and his three men sat at a corner table and there was a bottle and glasses on the table but they weren't drinking. Burdett had his hands on the top of the table, idly rolling a cigar between his fingers; the other three had their hands down out of sight.

Shag said, "I wonder what they're holdin', boss."

"Give you a guess."

"I already guessed. I'll take the pinch-faced one on the left; I never did like him anyway."

"Then I'll take the one on the right," Gunnison said, and looked at Shag, seeing a cool young man, a little afraid, but still cool.

"We'll take care of the ones in the middle when we get to 'em, huh?"

Gunnison smiled and stepped inside, losing himself for a moment in the crowd that always seemed to congregate near the door. He started to motion Shag away from him, then saw that the young man had already done so and it told Gunnison that this young man had known this kind of trouble before. He pushed through the crowd and exited in view of Burdett's table and they saw him and all motion stopped.

Gunnison said, "You want to call the turn, Burdett?"

A flicker of the eye warned him and he drew and fired in one motion, yet at the same time turned aside as one of the men opened fire from under the table. Shag's sawed-off rifle blasted and took them by surprise; a man was flung out of his chair and another man got up and reeled for a step then fell. All the time Burdett held his hands on the table.

Four shots had been fired then the remaining man threw his hands high over his head and sat that way, his eyes round, his pistol on the floor where he had dropped it.

Gunnison glanced at the rent in his coat sleeve, then walked over to Burdett, who didn't move at all.

The saloon was completely quiet and Gunnison could hear his boots mulching the sawdust.

9

It was only after a thing like this that a man could put together what actually happened; it moved too fast to understand but the aftermath was always still, always silent. The man on Burdett's right had pulled the trigger first, but he wasn't used to shooting a gun under a table and Gunnison's sideward move had disturbed his aim; he never had a chance to fire a second time.

Shag stood there holding his rifle; there was blood on his hip where a bullet had raked him, and the man who had nicked him lay dead in the sawdust. Burdett remained at the table, his hands still, while the third man remained standing, his hands high over his head; his eyes were round and he kept swallowing heavily.

To him Gunnison said, "Get on your horse and get the hell out of here."

There was no hesitation and with a look of gratitude the man bent and started to pick up his fallen gun.

"Leave it!" Shag said and the man did; he hurried out and a moment later they heard his horse, then the saloon was quiet again.

The swinging doors parted and Hank Freeman came in, still wearing his bartender's apron. He looked at everything and said nothing.

Burdett was watching Charlie Gunnison and they stared at each other for a moment, then Gunnison said, "I hate a man who don't have guts enough to fight his own fight."

"It wasn't my fight," Burdett said.

"How did I know where to find you?"

Burdett shrugged. "You tell me."

"Your cook knew where you'd be," Gunnison said. "I got the message. I'm here. And I'm waiting."

"Waiting for what?"

"You dared me to come after you," Gunnison said. "I'm here." He waited a moment; Burdett started to reach for a cigar, then thought better of it. Every man in the saloon waited and their breathing was a gentle, soft sound in the stillness. Gunnison got tired of waiting; he said, "Burdett, no one rustles Skillet beef. Not and get away with it."

"I never put a rope on your damned steers," Burdett snapped.

"You knew it was being done. Tell me I'm a liar."

"And get shot?" He shook his head.

"You're no man, Burdett. No man at all. You want to know what you are? A big loud-mouthed tub of guts. All talk, a big wind blowing. And nothing at all behind it." Burdett clenched his fists and looked at them. "Tell me that ain't so." He waited and Burdett said nothing. "Tell it to these men in this room so they'll know they're wrong, that you're more than a nothing sitting there."

Burdett banged his fist against the table and growled in his throat. "You want me to draw," he said. "You want to kill me." He shook his head violently. "I'm not going to commit suicide."

"So you're going to sit there, backed down, a big mouth with nothing to back you up?"

"I'm not goin' to get shot," Burdett said. "By you or by him." He looked at Shag and the sawed-off rifle.

"Stand up," Gunnison said.

Burdett did not move and Gunnison suddenly grasped the edge of the table and flung it away, scattering whiskey and discarded playing cards; Burdett remained in his chair, looking at Gunnison.

"Now, damn it, get up!"

Hank Freeman said, "I don't want you shooting cold meat, Charlie."

"I'm not goin' to shoot him," Gunnison said. "Take off your gunbelt, Burdett. Throw it away."

"What for?"

"Do it!"

"You'd better, mister," Shag said softly. "I don't think he'll tell you again."

Burdett frowned. "With fists?" He smiled. "You want to fight with fists, Gunnison?"

"If the idea doesn't scare you."

He laughed then and shucked his gunbelt and gave it a toss. "Hell, I'd like it," he said and jumped the interval while Gunnison was reaching his belt buckle. The move caught him with his hands busy, but he pivoted and let Burdett's rush bounce off him; he dropped his gun by stepping out of his chaps and kicking them to one side.

Burdett was squared off and he moved in, fast, his feet kicking sawdust and he swung with both fists; one Gunnison let bounce off his shoulder and the other knocked his hat off as he went under Burdett and hit him hard just over the belt.

Gunnison was as tall as Burdett, but lighter boned, and faster on his feet. He kept whirling and hitting Burdett and taking a little punishment to do it, but he took the sting out of the man's fists by backing away from the blows, all the time punching to the heart until Burdett's breathing grew labored and his eyes were wide.

For two minutes they circled and threw fists at each other and there was no man watching who didn't see that Gunnison was getting Burdett to waste himself, throw himself away. He got hit a little to do it but it was a price he wanted to pay, a small cut on the cheek and another over the eye.

Burdett was slowing down; his feet sluggishly kicked the sawdust and he was panting and Gunnison then decided that he'd carried the man far enough; he cocked his fist and exploded it in Burdett's face, driving the man back into the men lining the bar. They caught him and propelled him back and Gunnison met him, stopping him with a driving blow under the heart, dropping him with one he brought up from the floor.

Then he walked over and put on his chaps, fastening the buckle in back. He looked at Burdett and said, "Does this man have any friends here?" Some looked at each other and Gunnison pointed to them. "Take care of him then." His glance touched Shag and they went out together, Shag limping a little. A crowd lined the porch and they passed through. Gunnison said, "Where's the doctor's office?"

"The other part of town," Shag said.

"We'll have him take a look at you."

"Hardly worth the while."

"We'll do it just the same," Gunnison said.

The doctor's office was dark and Gunnison knocked several times before a light showed; the doctor pulled back the lace curtain, held up the lamp and looked at them through the glass. Then he saw the blood on Shag's hip and opened the door.

"Didn't know who it was," he said. "My office is right off the hall." He handed the lamp to Gunnison then went in and put a match to several others. "Get up there on the table, young fella. Drop your pants."

He washed his hands and put on his glasses and examined the wound. "Nothing much," he said. "Three stitches ought to close it." He washed the wound and got his instruments and then said, "I heard some shooting in Sintown awhile ago. This part of it?"

"Yep," Shag said. "The other two won't be comin' here."

"I don't suppose it's any of my business what it was about," the doctor said.

"No, it ain't," Gunnison said, "but I'll tell you. Burdett's men, along with a few from Dannon's thought they'd rustle a few head of Skillet stock. They didn't. Burdett came to town and invited me to join him."

"Burdett's dead?"

"No," Gunnison told him. "He didn't do any shooting."

"You've been busy," the doctor said and made the final stitch on Shag's hip. He bandaged him tightly and the young man pulled up his pants and swung his legs to the floor. "I heard about Henry Stiles," the doctor said. "He never pulled a gun on anyone."

"I know that," Gunnison admitted.

"Yet he's dead." The doctor shook his head. "How's a thing like that ever made right?"

"I don't know," Gunnison said solemnly. "But if I can ever prove that Stiles really didn't have a gun, I'll bring Big Sam in for killing him."

The doctor looked at him steadily. "You'd do that?"

"Wouldn't the old man do that?"

"Yes, he would have."

"How much?" Gunnison asked.

"What? Oh, two dollars."

Gunnison paid him and they went out and stood on the dark walk for a minute. A man walked toward them and when he drew near they saw that it was Hank Freeman; he struck a match, not only to light his cigar, but to give them a look at his face.

"Burdett didn't think it was going to go that way," he said. "He wasn't alone in this, I suppose?" He puffed on his cigar and waited, then said, "I guess if I was in your place I'd have done the same. Some men have to fear a brand to get along with it. Still it's a shame. Trouble's not good."

"You're walkin' all around your point," Gunnison pointed out.

Freeman laughed softly. "Ain't I though. Consider the town, Charlie. You know, they've got rights. A range war will split 'em wide open."

"There won't be any," Gunnison promised.

"You sound sure."

"It takes two to fight."

Freeman's manner sobered. "Are you telling me Skillet won't fight?"

"I'm saying that Spike and Star won't. This has been a warning to Burdett and Dannon. They won't get another." He slapped Shag on the arm. "Let's ride."

"Damn it, Charlie, I don't want to see any outfit makin' the law," Freeman said. "If there's trouble, I'll—"

"You're not always around," Gunnison said. "Goodnight."

They walked down the street to their horses, untied them and swung up and they were in no hurry now; they let the horses walk and Shag dozed in the saddle, his head tipped forward, his body riding loose and easy.

Gunnison was tired, but he held off sleep, thinking all the while about this night and just what he could expect of it. George Dannon and Kyle Burdett had taken a chance and he didn't blame them for it; they had to find out just how tight Skillet was going to be run. The price was a little high but they had known the risks, accepted them, believing all the while that they wouldn't have to pay much, not really.

Only it hadn't worked out that way and now they'd mind their own business for a few months until the lesson wore off. It wasn't over Gunnison knew, for he'd seen this pattern before; men always forgot and came back for more or figured that their luck would change the next time; whatever the reason, they always came back again.

During the next two weeks Gunnison spent a good deal of time away from the ranch house, riding over Rainsford's vast range, checking on things personally. Gator often rode with him, and occasionally Shag came along; Gunnison liked the young man, liked him because he was good with stock, not lazy, and kept a closed mouth.

With the passing days, Gunnison began to feel more at home with the problems and advantages of so much land and had already made up his mind what kind of a shipment he meant to make in the fall, what he wanted to sell and keep; it was a paring down yearly and if done right, a man could take advantage of range land and market conditions and turn a better profit.

Early rains had filled the watersheds and the creeks would be good until late August and the grass was thick and if the market held, he'd ship early and heavy and bank a big year. But in his mind he formed alternate plans in case the summer turned out to be a grass-burner or if the creeks went dry earlier than usual; a man had to figure on these things and be ready to move while there was time. If he rounded up early, and sold early, before the market got flooded, he could come out all right. Wait a bit too long and he'd lose his shirt.

His days were filled with little problems; Big Sam got into a fight with one of the men and that had to be settled, Dal was getting dry and Gator had to go to town and get him, dragging him out of Prairie Belle's place and back to the ranch.

Gunnison lived in the big house and Letty Shannon was the only one who spoke to him; Lana Rainsford ignored him and went out of her way to avoid him and he didn't let this bother him, and that bothered her.

She went to town often and spent her two thousand dollars on foolishness and he made no attempt to stop her, but when it was gone she discovered that she could not get any more; the banker wouldn't give her a penny without the judge's permission and the judge asked Gunnison, who said, "No."

He was not surprised when she came into his study, her manner milder than usual. She wore a white dress that displayed her good shoulders and when she spoke, the angry shrillness was gone from her voice.

"Mr. Gunnison, I simply must talk to you."

"Getting lonesome?"

She was not and she almost told him so, but she changed her mind. "Yes, to be honest about it. I'd like to go to Chicago for a month."

"It'll be hot in Chicago. Very high humidity there in June."

"I've been to Chicago," she said.

"Then go someplace else. San Francisco."

"I've been there."

He shrugged. "Kansas City? Boston? New York? No? You've been to all those places?" He looked at her. "Then you ought to spend the summer here. If you're good I'll let you paint the inside of the house."

"Don't play with me!"

He laughed. "I'd rather play with a rattler shedding his skin. You want some money so you can gad around and play the big lady. Well, the answer is no."

"You have no right!"

"Now you know better than that."

She almost lost her temper, but she managed to remain sweet and smiling. "You must miss your wife. Heaven knows when she'll get here. I've heard that it's not easy for a man, once he's been married." She stood up, her skirt rustling. "I'll bet I get the money. Want to bet?" She arched an eyebrow at him, then laughed and left the room.

He watched her go, then a moment later Letty Shannon stepped into the room; she said nothing but he knew that she had heard it all and wondered what she was thinking.

10

He took the buggy to town to meet the five o'clock train; the day was smotheringly hot, and not a breath of air stirred and as he stood on the depot platform in the useless shade he could see the heat shimmer off the rails and when he saw the train it seemed to move along under a blanket of its own smoke.

The engine came into the station, breathing hot steam and spewing cinders and passed a little beyond and still he could smell hot oil and the pungent coal smoke. The conductor stepped down with his wooden step and placed it so the passengers could alight, then Gunnison saw her and moved forward, gently pushing through the thin crowd.

He would have kissed her, only he knew that it would embarrass her; he simply put his arm around her and took her satchels and led her to the buggy. She was a small woman in her late twenties, fat with child now and bothered by the heat; as soon as she got in the rig she took off her hat and tried to do something with her hair.

"It must have been a long, tiring trip for you," he said gently, adjusting the top well forward so that it shaded her face and upper body. Then he turned the team and started back, driving slowly. She loosened the tight bodice of her traveling dress and leaned her head against his shoulder.

"Have we a nice place?" she asked.

"A very big house," he said. "But we're just guests in it. When this is done with we'll have enough money to build what we want."

"And lose it again?"

"People are always winning and losing something," he told her. "You're not afraid, are you?"

"A little," she said. "A strange country, and things make me nervous now that didn't use to bother me." She looked at him with her round, brown eyes and round sweet face. "Has it been bad for you, Charlie? I suppose that's silly to ask; it's always very bad before they send for you."

"It's turned off quiet," he said and let it go at that.

"I wish we were alone in this house," she said, then shook her head. "It's a hard thing to decide, isn't it? I didn't want to be alone when the baby came, and still I didn't want to come so far, in a strange country."

"You came because I wanted you with me," Gunnison said. "And that's as it should be." He reached out and patted her hand. "I don't think it would be wise to trust Lana Rainsford, Betty. But Letty Shannon, the old man's ward, is all right."

"I suppose she's pretty?" She looked at him intently, then smiled. "It's the kind of a thing a pregnant woman thinks of, Charlie. Pay no attention to it."

"I always pay attention to you," he said, then saw the riders on the road and watched them come on until they were close enough to recognize.

Fields Carlyle pulled up, he had two men with him and one

of them smiled at Charlie Gunnison. "Remember me, Charlie? McKitrick."

"Yes, how are you, Joel." He shook hands with the man then introduced his wife and they were all very mannerly with their hats and smiles.

"It's a mighty hot day," Carlyle said. "But in some respects it's cooler. Wouldn't you say so, Charlie?"

"I'm inclined to go along with that," Gunnison admitted. "You've lived a time in this country. So tell me, do you think the weather will hold out the summer?"

"I would say so," Carlyle said. He looked at McKitrick and the other man and they nodded. "However you've always got to figure that weather will go just so long and then it has to change. Usually a storm."

"Well, it'll be something to watch for," Gunnison said. He nodded to them and lifted the reins and they touched the brim of their hats and bowed slightly to his wife and he drove on.

"My," Betty said, "they were polite. Are they friends of yours?"

"Let's just say they're not enemies, and I'm thankful for that." He looked at her and smiled. "They're the kind of men other men leave alone unless they want more trouble than they can handle."

They drove on through the heat of the day, following the gentle dip and rise of the road and in time they came to the pole arch and the road leading to the main ranch buildings, visible in the distance.

When they pulled into the yard, Shag came from the barn and helped Betty Gunnison down, then took her satchels. Gunnison tied the team and stepped onto the porch as Letty Shannon came out; she looked at Betty Gunnison and smiled. "I'm so very glad you're here." She took her inside to the parlor; it seemed cooler there because the curtains had been drawn and the thick walls kept the heat out.

Shag knew where to take the luggage and he went on down the hall and Letty went to the kitchen and came back with a large pitcher of iced tea. When Gunnison's wife saw this, she stared a moment, then said, "Ice? Why, I can't believe it. Ice in July!"

"Years ago Mr. Rainsford dug a large ice cellar," Letty said. "Every winter we have ice sawed from the creek and stored there and covered with four foot of sawdust." Then she laughed. "It's always a pleasant surprise to have ice in the summer. Here, let me take your duster. I've had a bath drawn; after you've had your tea you can rest."

"That's very thoughtful," Betty said. "Thank you."

Letty's glance touched Charlie Gunnison. "Lana went riding early this morning. She didn't say when she would be back or where she was going."

"I'll talk to Gator about it later," he said, and touched his wife on the shoulder. "Why don't you go with Letty; she'll show you your room and you can rest. I'll see you at supper."

He knew she wanted him to stay with her, and yet she understood that he couldn't; he had things to do, difficult things, so she smiled and he bent and kissed her gently, then went out.

Letty sat down and picked up her glass of tea and she waited a moment before she said anything, as though waiting for Betty Gunnison to start a conversation. Then she realized that she'd have to do it and said, "I know how difficult it is to come to someone else's house; I had to do it years ago when Mr. Rainsford took me in and no matter how much you're made to feel wanted, you never get over the feeling that you're really not . . . well, one of the family."

"You're very understanding."

"I want us to be friends," she said. "I think it's the only way we'll be able to live. Your husband can live surrounded by enemies and I admire him for it, but I'm not that way and I don't think any woman is. We need security. Do you understand me?"

"Yes," Betty Gunnison said. "And I'm sure we'll be friends." She finished her tea and got up. "Do you run the house?"

"I have been. Why don't we manage it together?"

"That might be nice," she said.

Letty smiled. "I'll show you your room. Your bath is waiting."

They went into the large hall and Betty Gunnison looked at the high ceiling and the staircase and said, "It's a very big house. Where does my husband—?"

"He's been using Mr. Rainsford's study," Letty said. "But he'll move now." At the end of the hall she opened a door and stood back. "Will you call me if you need anything? There's a bell pull connected to the kitchen."

"Yes," she said and went in and closed the door; Letty stood there until the lock clicked, then she walked on to the back of the house.

Lana Rainsford sat under an oak tree; her horse was tied in a thicket deep in the grove, out of sight. She was not readily visible, sitting in the shadows that way, her brown riding clothes blending well with the background. She kept watching to the east and then she saw a horseman top a small rise and come on toward the grove and ten minutes later George Dannon swung down.

He looked around, taking an eye sweep of the land, then he drew her to him and kissed her, holding her a long moment before letting her go. Then they sat down and George Dannon said, "What's the big man doing these days?"

"Gunnison?" She shrugged. "Running a ranch. He knows his business."

"I haven't seen Sam and Dal in town."

"They're not allowed in town," Lana said.

Dannon made a face. "No man would keep me from doin' what I wanted to do."

"Is that so? I thought Gunnison threw down on you in your own house and—"

"Never mind that," he said quickly. "I told you what happened; he took me by surprise."

"You were waiting for him, weren't you?"

He made a cutting motion with his hand. "Damn it, I said I didn't want to talk about it."

She laughed because she had him sore and it pleased her. "You've let things grow quiet, George. I don't know how much good that will do. I thought you were going to push him. That's what you told me you were going to do, push him from all directions."

"Damn it, you know what happened. With a man like him you've got to be smarter than usual. I'm working on something now, but it'll take money. More than I have."

"Well, I don't have any," Lana said and pursed her lips. "He won't give me any either."

"Sam and Dal still have theirs, haven't they?"

She frowned, then nodded. "What are you thinking of now, George?"

"Let me ask you a question. If I got my men together and Kyle Burdett threw in his bunch and we rode on Skillet, what do you think would happen?"

"You'd get shot to pieces," Lana said. "Somehow Gunnison's managed to take hold, get the crew behind him. They trust him. Yes, they'd cut you both up."

"And if Carlyle joined me?"

"You might do it then," she said, "but Carlyle won't. He'll wait and after you've all broken your backs trying, he'll step in and take it all."

"So it wouldn't be any use to make little trouble for Skillet," George Dannon said. "To whip Gunnison he's got to have a kind of trouble he can't fight."

"What kind would that be?"

Dannon stretched out on the grass. "Gunnison didn't like it when Stiles was killed. He didn't like it at all."

"Who did?" Lana asked. "It was stupid of Sam no matter how it really happened."

"Maybe, but it happened and it's real interestin', how Gunnison took it, gettin' kind of steamed up over it." He turned his head and looked at her. "I think he'd forgive a man like Stiles for taking a calf if it meant the difference between eating and starving."

"What are you getting at, George?"

"I'd like to talk to Sam and Dal," he said. "Where are they?"

"They're living in that line shack about four miles northwest of here," she said. "Gunnison stuck them up there in the rough country out of pure meanness."

"You tell 'em I want to talk over something," Dannon said.

"Now?"

"Is there a better time?"

"I wouldn't get back to the ranch until well after dark," Lana said.

He laughed. "Afraid of the dark?"

"Would you ride part of the way with me, George?"

"Sure," he said. "And one of these days we'll ride together any time we please." He sat up and scratched his back. "May's not easy to live with. Sometimes we go for days without speakin'. I don't try to make it easier either because one of these days I'll put a thousand dollars in her hand and tell her to catch a train and I want her to be eager to do it. That'll be the day when you and I can—"

"That'll be the day all right," Lana Rainsford said. "George, you've been saying that for a year now."

"And I mean it," he said. "A man can only move so fast in these things. Hell, you wouldn't want her to get wind of anything, now would you?"

"I've felt like going to her and telling her good," Lana said.

He showed a brief alarm. "That would be pretty stupid. We've got things our way, Lana."

"What do you think that comes to? Love under the trees?"

"Ah, Lana—"

"Ah, hell," she said, getting up. "I'll tell Sam and Dal to expect you. When?"

"I'll follow you in twenty minutes or so."

She looked at him. "There's only one thing wrong with you, George: I never know what you're thinking."

"Do you have to?"

"It would help," she said evenly, "to really know what you

thought about me. I know all of the things you want, George, and after you get them I wonder how much I'll mean to you."

She walked back and got her horse and rode from the grove, striking off in a northerly direction and he watched her go and when she passed from sight he got up, mounted his horse and rode in the other direction.

As he breasted a rise he stopped and got down; Kyle Burdett was stretched out on the ground, a hand over his eyes. He squinted at George Dannon and said, "You could have found a spot with some shade." Then he sat up. "How did you make out, or shouldn't I have asked?"

"She's going to fix it so I can see Sam and Dal."

Burdett didn't seem much impressed with the idea; he shrugged and rolled a cigaret. Dannon squatted and said, "Why not? It's their place, ain't it? Why shouldn't they foot the bill?" He laughed softly. "What do you want? Spend our money? Not me. I tell you, Kyle, I've got the answer." He stood up. "You wait and see."

"What else have I got to do?" Burdett asked. "I'm not facing him straight out, you can bet on that. I don't like the idea of dying and I came damned close to it."

"You really thought he'd back down when you called him out?"

"Wouldn't you have? How did he know how many men I had with me?" He shook his head. "I really never thought he'd show."

"He did," Dannon said. "Well, here's to some sweet talk. I'll let you know, Kyle. In the morning." He stepped into the saddle and turned north and before he dipped over the rise he looked back and saw that Burdett was riding back toward his place and Dannon smiled, feeling pretty pleased with himself.

11

Dal Rainsford did the cooking because Big Sam always burned the bacon and his pancakes were soggy in the middle and his coffee was either too weak or too strong. The line shack was nestled in some trees near a creek that tumbled and plunged down a rocky course; they were near the mouth of a small canyon that led to two sections of badlands. Carlyle's place was two miles north and somewhat of a fence separated the two outfits and it was their job to keep cattle from breaking through, to keep cattle down in the low country during the summer for the badlands was a winter haven for the herd, shelter when the weather turned off severe.

Sam was at the creek getting water when he saw his sister making slow progress up the trail. He called to Dal, who came out, and they stood there while she came on and swung down. The sun was down behind the hills, yet the day held a bake-oven heat; she wiped sweat from her face with a handkerchief and loosened further the buttons of her shirt.

"George Dannon's on his way here," she said. "He wants to talk to you."

"What about?" Sam asked.

"He'll tell you." She took the dipper from the water pail Sam held and drank deeply.

Dal Rainsford said, "Where did you see George?"

"On the range," she said. "I ran across him while I was riding." She looked at her brother. "Well, he's a neighbor. Isn't it all right to talk to a neighbor?"

"It'd be a lot better if we didn't have anything to do with George Dannon," Dal said flatly. "The old man never trusted him and I can't say as I ever did either."

"Well, it won't hurt to talk to him," Lana said. "Is that supper I smell?" She walked inside and pushed some gear off a chair and sat down. "Don't you ever sweep this place?"

"It suits us," Big Sam said defensively.

Dal put out another plate and knife and fork, then they sat down to eat. Finally Big Sam said, "How long are we goin' to have to stay here? All summer?"

"Until Gator tells you to come down," she said. "And behave yourself, will you? Acting like little kids doesn't change anything."

Dal went on eating, but Big Sam stopped and looked carefully at her. "That's kind of a change in tune for you, ain't it? I mean, you told me you was goin' to raise so much hell he'd be glad to send you away. Didn't work out, huh?" He laughed. "I didn't think he had a soft spot."

"He has," Lana said, "and he took a buggy to town today to get her." She looked at each of them. "His wife, pregnant and all. I got that much out of Letty."

"So?" Sam said.

Lana smiled. "You just don't understand a jealous woman, Sam. That's because you're a man and can't know what a pregnant woman thinks." Her laugh was a soft bubble of sound. "Here we are, living in the same house, a wife with a big belly and me with a closet full of clothes and a figure to show them off."

Dan Rainsford said, "Lana, I wouldn't do that. I wouldn't fight him that way."

"I do the best I can, the only way I can," she snapped. "Do you understand? I want out. I want him out so I can get my money out of the place and go east." She raised her head when she heard a horseman coming toward them. "That'll be George."

They got up and went out and Dannon crossed the creek and dismounted. He smiled and hitched up his pants and sniffed. "That smells good. Mighty good."

"We just finished supper," Sam said. "What you want, George?"

"Why, some talk," Dannon said. "No harm in that."

"Depends on what you want to talk about," Dal said.

"It seems to me we've got something in common," Dannon said. "None of us want Gunnison here."

"So what of it?" Dal asked.

"So I say get rid of him."

Sam laughed and Dal Rainsford shrugged. "As far as I'm concerned I'm willing to wait. In two years he'll leave and the place will be a quarter mine. Why break my head?"

"That seems like a long time," Dannon said. "I've figured out a way to do it quicker, but it'll take money." He looked at each of them. "Say, two thousand apiece. We'll go partners on it."

"Partners in what?" Big Sam asked.

"You don't want to hear it," Dal told him. "George, the old man never liked you and that's one thing he did that I agreed with. Why don't you let the Rainsfords grind their own ax?"

"You could at least listen to a man," Dannon said.

"That's right," Lana said. "At least listen."

Sam was ready; it was Dal that hesitated, then he shrugged and they all went inside. George Dannon was smiling again.

Gunnison normally left the house a little after dawn each day and returned after dark, long after the supper hour and usually he would have something brought to the study, then he would go to the rooms he shared with his wife. The heat was bad and being away from her for so much was bad, and yet he could do nothing about either thing; he thought she understood, tried to understand, and he knew that neither succeeded.

She knew that he wanted to make enough money so they could start over and she knew that he loved her and wanted to be with her, yet the loneliness was still there and everything that took him away from her grew out of proportion in her mind and she fought it without much success.

There were times when she could not suppress her feelings and she could not talk to him without crying. He would comfort her and tell her that she was tired and to go to the study to sleep on the cot.

It was these times that made him think it would be better

to pack their things and leave and let Skillet go to the wolves. Then he would think about it and think of Stiles, who died over nothing, and he knew that he couldn't do it. He would have to stay. To leave would throw a door open to a large scale range war in which a lot of people would get hurt.

He lay on the cot, clad in the bottom half of his underwear. His window was open, hoping for a night breeze to spring up, and there was a good moon, bright in the clearest of dark skies. There was a sound in the hall; someone moved there, but he paid no attention to it until his door opened and he sat up.

Lana Rainsford stood there. She had on a thin dressing gown that lay clingingly against the smooth roundness of her hips and flat stomach, and she smiled at him.

"I couldn't sleep," she said softly and started to step inside. Her eyes were on Gunnison and she did not see Letty Shannon at all until Letty moved against her and rammed her in the pit of the stomach with her elbow.

Lana grunted and stepped back. Letty looked at her and said, "You must be sleep walking, Lana. Go back to bed now."

"What are you talking about?"

"Just go back to bed," Letty said again and pushed against her. Lana stepped back into the hall, then she swore softly and wheeled around. She took three steps, then stopped and laughed and Gunnison got up and came to the door and looked out.

His wife was standing farther down; she had on a white dressing gown and she made no move at all for a moment. Then she wheeled and hurried back to her room.

Lana said, "Well, I didn't lose after all, did I?"

"You didn't win anything either," Letty said. She waited and Lana shrugged and went on to her room. After the door closed, she said, "I'm sorry. Really sorry."

"You don't suppose she thinks—"

"Who knows what a woman thinks," Letty said. "I'll talk to her."

"It's my place—"

"I'll talk to her," she repeated. "Men say the wrong things sometimes. They protest too much that they're innocent."

He watched her go on down the hall and when she went into Betty Gunnison's room, he closed the door and sat down on his cot, feeling like swearing and knowing that it wouldn't do any good.

He waited thirty minutes, then an hour, hoping she would come to him or that Letty would come back and tell him it was all right, but no one came. Finally he fell asleep.

The next morning he went to her room early; she was sleeping, her nightgown awry, and she woke when she heard his step, woke and looked at him wide-eyed for an instant. He sat down on the edge of her bed and said, "Betty, we've got to get away from this place. I mean it. To hell with the money."

She shook her head. "I thought that last night, but now I know differently. Charlie, I'm sorry I've been a burden to you. I see that I have. And I can see that I'm being driven and I don't like that. I never did." She sat up and then went to the washstand and put water on her face. After she dried, she turned to him. "Letty told me the truth. I know it's the truth because I know you, Charlie. But if she hadn't told me, I would have—" She shrugged her shoulders. "Well, I really don't know what I'd have believed. But I'm not going to be driven away, Charlie. I can fight too."

He came to her and put his arms around her and kissed her. "Then let's get some breakfast. I don't want you fighting on an empty stomach."

"All right," she said, smiling. "And, Charlie, no more sleeping in the study."

In the early fall, Charlie Gunnison had made up his mind about shipping and during the roundup he was away for weeks at a time and he didn't want to be. The baby was due in eight weeks and he worried about that, in spite of Betty's assurance that everything was all right.

Skillet had stopped losing calves after the gunfight at the

fence and there was no hint of trouble from either Dannon or Burdett, but Gunnison was not fooled into believing it was ended. Now and then Fields Carlyle rode over to talk, and twice Gunnison went to Carlyle's place. He liked the man in spite of his isolationism. Carlyle would simply not allow himself to be pulled into anything.

There was a touch of snow in October, an unusual thing and from the older hands who knew weather, Gunnison gathered that there was a hard winter ready to come down from the north and it helped him make his decision. The range was overstocked and he decided that he had been right in his decision to ship early and sell off heavy. Gator agreed and got the crew together for the drive into the railhead while Gunnison arranged terms with the cattle buyer who came down from Denton.

The market was holding steady but Gunnison suspected that it was going to drop, and drop fast, as soon as other ranchers realized they'd have to do a lot of hand feeding over the winter. He wanted to sell now, to take advantage of the good market, and then push what was left of the cattle into the badlands early so they'd find shelter. He would also have to buy feed and haul it to the ranch; it took time to handle a severe winter, and the man who waited until the first real cold snap to do it usually lost more cattle than he could afford.

The drive to the railhead came at a bad time; Betty was nearly due to deliver her child and Gunnison wanted to be there, but couldn't; a drive without the boss along was no drive at all; it was a custom that had to be honored if he meant to hold the crew's respect.

When he left the ranch, Letty promised to look after everything, and Gunnison was some relieved, although he thought he had it figured out in his mind. It would take two days to drive to the railhead, a small junction eight miles west of town; once the cattle were in the yards and tallied, he could get the doctor and come back.

That would be time enough.

But he hadn't counted on a sopping rain that hit them

late in the afternoon of the first day, turning the prairie into a mire and swelling the creeks. That added another half day on the drive and when he got there he found no cattle cars waiting; there had been a washout to the east and the train would be delayed a day and a half.

The cattle buyer didn't want to tally twice; he wanted it taken as the cattle went up the chute to the cars and Gunnison didn't blame him, so he went along with it. But he sent Shag on into town to take the doctor out to the ranch. Late that night Shag came back and said that the doctor was not there; some trainmen had been hurt in the derailment and no one knew for sure when the doctor would get back.

The train arrived even later than expected and Gunnison drove the crew to the point of exhaustion loading the cars. He sent Shag back to town and worried until the job was done. Then he picked a fresh horse, changed his saddle and rode toward the ranch, not caring whether he wore the horse out or not.

The weather was turning nippy and late in the afternoon, when he crossed a creek, the horse broke through thin rime ice, and there was the smell of snow in the air. He adjusted his gait to match the horse's stamina and it was well after dark before he reached the ranch house. Flinging off, he dashed across the porch; there was no sign of the doctor's buggy, but then he supposed that Shag had put it in the barn and stabled the team.

The lamps were on in the hall and he looked for the servants, but they were not around. Then he saw Letty Shannon came out of his wife's room and he went to her.

"How's my wife?"

"Fine," Letty said, smiling.

"Where's the doctor?"

"In town I guess. Do you want to go in and see her?"

"What the hell do you think?" He put his hand on her shoulder and shook her slightly. "What are you smiling about?"

"You're a father."

"The hell you say!" He rushed past her, then paused at the end of the hall. "A boy or girl?"

"Ask your wife," Letty said and he went in.

She looked very tired and very happy and he went to her and sat on the edge of the bed and lifted the corner of the blanket-wrapped bundle she held against her breast.

He said, "He's red."

"It's a girl," she said. "Are you happy, Charlie?"

"Yes," he said and gently kissed her. "You're all right?"

"All right," she said. "Letty was with me. Will I ever be able to thank her?"

"When Letty does something," he said, "it isn't for thanks." He took her hand and held it. "Betty, in the spring we'll go."

"If your work is finished," she said.

"We'll go if it isn't."

"You finish this," she said. "I'm fine now. Really fine."

12

Gunnison went into town with the supply wagon; there was snow on the ground, a loose foot of it, and the way the weather was, a little warm turning off to cold nights, a hard icy crust would form making grazing difficult. That kind of weather made ranch work tough, for it put a man in the saddle and kept him there, chipping ice from the creeks and water holes, and hauling feed.

He left Shag at the store with another man and went to the bank, then he saw Carlyle and McKitrick ride in; they stopped and Carlyle spoke from the muffled folds of his coat. "Good weather for a drink. Join me?"

"Fine," Gunnison said. "I'll meet you in Sintown."

"The Best Place is where I usually drink," Carlyle said, and rode on. Gunnison went into the store to leave a personal order, then walked along the snow-covered walk, past the vacant lots and on to Fred Best's place.

He went in and saw a group huddled around the pot-bellied stove. Carlyle and McKitrick were at the bar and Gunnison joined them, unbuttoning his coat to let some of the room's heat get to him.

McKitrick said, "It'll go to zero tonight." He looked up as Hank Freeman came over. "Just set out a bottle and three glasses," he said and turned to Gunnison. "But I don't guess it's any worse than a Wyoming winter. Except there a man knows it's coming and usually gets ready for it."

Carlyle poured and they lifted their glasses. "Here's to a long winter."

"Maybe for you, but it can't thaw too soon for me," Gunnison said. "I like to see green grass." He turned around and hooked his elbows on the bar and looked around the room. "Drink and play cards. Some way to pass the time."

"You could go over to Poker Ann's and have fun with the girls," Carlyle said. "But that's not your style, Charlie. Not mine either." He put his elbows on the bar and stood that way, his shoulders hunched, his head thrust forward. "I understand that Dannon didn't ship many and Burdett didn't ship at all. That wasn't too smart."

"I let a man run his own business," Gunnison said, "as long as it doesn't interfere with mine." He stopped talking as the door opened and Burdett stepped inside, followed by two of his men. They were nearly to the stove before they saw Gunnison, and Burdett stopped and stared, then unbuttoned his coat. He took off his gloves and spread his hands to the heat.

"I came in here for a drink and some cards, not trouble," he said, not looking at Gunnison.

"Do what you want," Gunnison said and turned his back to him. Hank Freeman still stood there, watching this. "How are Stiles' family making out?"

"Lean," Freeman said.

"I want them taken care of if you can do it without bringing Skillet into it. If the widow suspected—"

"Sure," Freeman said. "I can take care of it." He brushed a finger against his mustache. "You want to forget about the shooting?"

Gunnison raised his head quickly. "No. I don't want to let a thing like that go. You understand, Hank. It's not finished. A thing like that isn't finished until we get all the answers." He blew out a long breath and patted his pockets for makings and found none; Carlyle gave him a cigar and a match. He puffed a moment, his eyes squinted. "Sam's a wild one. The old man knew that and didn't like it. Maybe I've been too hard on him. If I brought him out of the badlands and gave him a chance to howl a little we'd find out more than we now know."

"I'll take care of the Stiles widow," Freeman said, and moved on down the bar to tend the customers. Gunnison finished his drink, thanked Carlyle for the cigar, and went out. After the door closed, Carlyle looked into the backbar mirror and saw Burdett had watched all this.

"When I see an ornery man sitting quietly," Carlyle said, "I just naturally get suspicious."

"That's the time for a man to mind his own business."

"True," Carlyle said. "Drink up and let's go."

November was a month of bland skies and weather holding steady, and each day contained an ominous threat. The noon sky was gray, like old lead, and there was little wind and no snow. Gunnison kept his men busy and they had pushed all the cattle into the badlands a month before and hauled in hay and feed, using three wagons continually for a solid week.

Then the weather broke, howling down from the north, full of snow and gale winds, stripping the frozen prairie in spots and piling snow into huge, crusted drifts. Gunnison had his crew in the badlands, holed up in two line shacks that were supplied to last out the winter. Three men remained at the ranch to tend saddle stock and shovel snow from the house to the barn and keep doors battened down against the wild winds that blew for days at a time.

Shelter for men and animals became critical, for the temperature stayed around zero, and whipped by a howling wind, bit into exposed cheeks and nipped at the hands the minute heavy gloves were removed.

For nearly three weeks there was little activity, then the weather turned milder and the sun came out and the temperature hung just below freezing. This gave Gunnison and his crew a chance to repair storm damage, shingles ripped off by the wind, siding on the barn loosened, and if they had time, to dig a few more paths to the outbuildings.

Judge Caldwell surprised Charlie Gunnison by driving out to the ranch in his sleigh; Deputy Hank Freeman came with him and this made Gunnison suspicious. He invited Caldwell and Freeman into the house and seated them in the parlor while Charlie's wife brought coffee.

When they had soaked up a little heat, Gunnison said, "Is this business or pleasure, judge?"

He swished coffee around inside his mouth, then said, "Business, I'm afraid. Is Big Sam here?"

"No, he's in the hills."

Hank Freeman shook his head. "He ain't, Charlie. Big Sam came to town before the storm and put up at the hotel."

"Well, damn him—"

Caldwell held up his hand. "Charlie, I don't know how to tell you this exactly, but Big Sam and Lana sold their interest in Skillet. It's true. They've formed a company in town. Rented an office and everything. Call it Texas Development Company."

"Can they do that?" Gunnison asked. "The property doesn't become theirs, legally, until two years have—"

"Yes, I know all that," Caldwell said. "Charlie, they've thrown in with Dannon and Burdett. The old man left out a thing or two in his will, and someone's found the loopholes. You see, they might not own the property, but they could lease it until they did own it, then sell it. And that's what they're doing."

"Take a look at this," Freeman said, taking a folded notice from his inside coat pocket.

Gunnison read it; he'd read many of them before, the come-on notice for farmers, promising them good land, at cleap prices, with no Indian trouble connected with it.

"By the time the first thaw hits," Freeman said, "you'll see 'em gettin' off the trains, or arriving by wagons."

"Farmers on Skillet range?" Gunnison said. "They'll cut it up, plow the grass under and—"

"And you'd better not ride on them," Judge Caldwell said. "This company is all legal and proper, and as potential heirs, Sam and Lana—"

"They may not live long enough to be heirs if they're with Dannon and Burdett," Gunnison snapped. He got up and called the servant. "Is Miss Rainsford in her room?"

"Yassuh."

"You tell her I want to see her."

The servant shook his head. "She don' wanna be disturbed, boss."

"You tell her that if she isn't down here in five minutes, I'll come and bring her down." He went back to his chair and sat down. "And I thought I had it licked this winter." He shook his head sadly. "I suppose the town likes the idea?"

Judge Caldwell shrugged. "Well, there was the Stiles affair and a lot of decent people in town thought it was a damned shame. And things have changed, too. There was a time when people liked the idea of one brand supporting everything, but they've seen how prosperous a community can be when it caters to farmers. A lot more peaceful, too." He stopped talking when he heard a woman's step in the hall, then Lana Rainsford stepped into the parlor.

She looked at Gunnison and waited for him to speak.

"So you sold out," he said.

"Yes I did. What are you going to do about it?"

"What do you think I should do?" Gunnison asked. "When you asked me for money, what did you intend to do with it? What did you do with your two thousand dollars?"

"I drew it out of the bank and kept it," she said. "I told you I'd get rid of you and I will, Charlie."

He leaned back in his chair and looked at her steadily. "Your father didn't sire much, did he? You and Sam and Dal."

"We never wanted to be like him," she said. "But he never understood that, and you don't understand it."

"Lana, we are what we're born to be. About six years ago I was hired to squire a German prince on a hunting trip, and I got to know him pretty well. If he'd had his choice he'd have stayed in Wyoming, but he knew what he had to do, so he went back to Germany to his wife, who'd been picked for him, and his life, which had been picked for him." He shook his head. "So you threw in with two thieves. Do you know what will happen, Lana? They'll eat you alive before they're through."

"I'm going to leave this house," she said.

"You're free to go, but think about it. If you leave it, you won't ever come back."

"Do you think so?" She laughed softly. "Charlie, there are a lot of ways to fight you. This is mine. I want it and I mean to have it."

"You're a fool," Gunnison told her. "Dannon and Burdett will never let you have an acre of it. Tell me, how much did they put up in cash?" He watched her face and knew the truth without her answer. "Pack your things. Gator can take you into town."

"They're packed," she said. "I was only waiting for the weather to break." She walked to the arch and stopped there. "I don't know why I bother to tell you this, but Dal didn't go along with this. Just Sam and I."

She turned and walked back to her room and for a moment no one said anything; the judge broke the silence. "I'm glad the old man's not alive to see this. It would be interesting to know what Burdett and Dannon are up to. Sending out these land notices and bringing in farmers seems to me to be just a bother he'll have to tend to in time." Then he stopped talking and raised his head, looking squarely at Gunnison. "Is he after war between Skillet and these farmers?"

"Why not?" Freeman said. "He hasn't got the guts to fight it himself." He got up and stretched. "We'd best start back, judge." He put on his coat and hat. "Charlie, there won't be any stopping these farmers now. They've leased land and they're entitled to work it. I wouldn't want to see you stepping outside the law."

"Do you think I ought to allow Skillet range to be cut up, plowed under?"

Judge Caldwell frowned. "Charlie, you just can't kill 'em off." He tucked in his wool muffler and tugged on his gloves. "I don't know what to tell you to do, but I think it's important for you to remember that you must keep the good will of the people behind you. I know you could take a crew and burn out a few places and perhaps shoot some innocent people, and you could regain every bit of power the old man ever had, but it wouldn't last, Charlie. It may be that Skillet will never again be as big as it once was."

"There's a lot of land here," Freeman said. "A little bit here and a little bit there—" He waved his hands in a futile gesture. "It's a damned shame, that's what it is. It always hurts to see open range fenced."

Gunnison went to the door with them and watched them leave, then he called Gator and told him to get a sled hitched and take Lana and her luggage to town. He saw Shag shoveling snow by the cookshack and called him over.

"I'm sending Gator into town. I want you to saddle up and bring Dal back from the line camp. He's been lonein' it up there."

There was the question in Shag's eyes, but he didn't ask it; he nodded and trotted back toward the barn, his burlap-wrapped boots padding in the snow.

After Shag rode out, Gator brought the sled from the barn and then Lana came out; the servant carried her bags and her trunks and put them in the sled. She stood on the porch a moment, fastening the buttons of her coat.

"I won't say goodbye because I'll be back," she said, looking at Gunnison. "The old man made a mistake, hiring you. It'll take more than a cheap gunfighter to keep me away from what's mine."

"Just what is yours?"

"Skillet is mine because he was my father," Lana said. "When you're gone, Charlie, I'll be back. George Dannon promised me that."

"He lied to you," Gunnison said. "When I'm gone he'll ride on the farmers and take Skillet for himself."

"That's a lie!"

"Lana, it'll be a sad day for you when you find out the truth. Now you'd better go."

Gator handed her into the sled and wrapped a heavy blanket around her feet, then got in and turned around, going across country toward town. Gunnison watched them until they cleared the yard, then went into the house and found Letty and his wife in the parlor.

He walked over to the pot-bellied stove and warmed his hands, saying nothing. Letty spoke: "She's the biggest fool ever. Dannon has a wife."

He turned his head and looked at her a moment, then said, "I don't think it's like that at all."

"Don't bet on it. Lana will do anything to have her own way." She poured some coffee and Gunnison came over and got a cup.

He said, "I wonder what held Dal back?"

"You'll have to ask him."

"I sent for him to do just that," Gunnison said. "If he's going to break with the brand, I want him to do it now." He drank some of his coffee and remained in deep thought for several minutes. "Like it or not, this is going to affect Fields Carlyle. I guess he'll have to choose a side."

Gunnison's wife had held silent, not wanting to push her husband toward a woman's thinking, but she could not hold back any longer. "Charlie, there can't be a war between Skillet and these farmers. You can't give these two greedy men what they want."

"I know. But suppose war is declared on me? What do I do then? If I show weakness—" He shook his head and finished his coffee and put the cup aside. "Well, it looks like a new hand's been dealt and Dannon and Burdett are holding good cards."

13

Dal Rainsford arrived late; the women had retired an hour earlier and Charlie Gunnison worked on the books until Gator came in, then they went to the parlor for some coffee and some planning for the coming spring. With a hard winter almost behind them and many ranchers in deep trouble, it might be a good time to buy up stock, fatten them and ship in the first of summer to take advantage of good beef prices.

Rainsford put his horse in the barn before coming to the house, and he knocked once before stepping inside. At the archway he stopped and said, "Shag told me you wanted to see me."

"Come in and sit down," Gunnison told him. "Lana and Sam are living in town."

"I figured that," Dal said. He was thinner, tougher, and three months growth of whiskers covered his face. His hands were scarred from unending hard work and his clothes needed patching badly.

"Kind of a rough winter," Gator commented.

"You didn't hear me complain," Dal Rainsford said. He had been out of tobacco for a month and the flavor of Gunnison's cigaret was getting to him, but he said nothing about it.

"Why aren't you in town with your brother and sister?" Gunnison asked.

"There's nothing there for me." He helped himself to the coffee and held the cup in his hands for a time as though drawing warmth from it. "Sam and I have said goodbye. I know he's going to come back with Dannon and Burdett. He knows where I'll be when the time comes."

"And where'll that be?" Gunnison asked.

"Here. With a rifle. Saying goodbye to Sam wasn't easy. We fought, like we've always fought. And I got licked, like I've always been licked. But he didn't get my money and I didn't go with him." He shrugged his thin shoulders. "Suddenly the old man's work meant something to me. Believe it or not, I'm ready to fight for it." He drank his coffee and put the cup aside. "I know what Sam thinks. But he's wrong. After they run you out, Dannon and Burdett will turn on him. They'll kill him and take it all for themselves."

"Suppose they don't run me out?" Gunnison asked.

"Why, I've been countin' on that," Dal Rainsford said.

Gator sat there, now and then glancing at Charlie Gunnison, waiting, and Gunnison remained silent for a time. Then he said, "Did you bring your gear back with you?"

"There ain't much left, except what I'm wearing."

"I can use a good right hand," Gunnison told him. "The grass will be starting to peek through in another month and there'll be farmers coming in on every train." He looked steadily at Dal Rainsford. "It's going to be a tough year, but I know your father faced a few in his time. This is something we'll have to handle."

"I can handle my part," Dal Rainsford said with assurance. He stood up and stretched. "You want me in the bunkhouse or what?"

"Better move back into the house," Gunnison said. "You'll own this place one of these days and you might as well find out how hard the saddle is to ride."

Gator thought it was the mildest spring he had ever seen, long sunny days that thawed the snow and bulged the creeks and brought the grass up thick and green, and it was a time of hard work, with every man in the saddle, bringing the cattle onto the summer range, and painting and fixing up and as soon as the road dried enough to get wagons through, three were hitched and taken to town to replenish the dwindled winter supplies.

Buying for a ranch the size of Skillet was a big job, and

an order for flour meant four barrels, two hundred pounds of beans, three hundred of bacon; it took two men four trips to carry the salt from the store to the wagons. Gunnison and his wife went into town because she had been shut in all winter and she wanted to take the baby to the doctor to make sure he wasn't coming down with anything, and Gunnison wanted to have a talk with the banker; he had a list of things he had to take care of, things that couldn't be put off.

He put the crew up at the hotel and took a room on the second floor and that evening they had dinner in the dining room and they were eating when Fields Carlyle came in with McKitrick and Pony Deal. Gunnison nodded and would have let it go at that, but his wife remembered them from her first day and insisted that they be invited to eat with them.

Carlyle was gracious about it and McKitrick was a man at ease anywhere; only the thin-faced Pony Deal, with his pair of pistols under his coat, seemed silent and reserved.

"I expected this thawing to flood my lower pasture," McKitrick said pleasantly, "but it ran off in the creeks. We'll have good grass and I think a mild summer." He looked at Betty Gunnison and smiled. "I hope you don't think all the winters are this bad."

"Wyoming has taught me a good deal about winters," she said. "I've seen it so cold that you thought your bones would crack."

"The horse business has some advantages," Carlyle said. He glanced at Gunnison. "I hope I'm not talking out of turn, Charlie, but there are some things shaping up that I don't like."

"I don't like them either," Gunnison said. "But what Sam is doing is legal; he can lease Skillet range but he can't sell it."

"So I understand. I saw Dal come in town with you. He didn't go with Sam?"

"No."

"Odd," Carlyle said softly. "He always toed the mark when Sam told him something."

"Not this time," Gunnison said. "Sam pushed him too far once too often."

Carlyle shrugged. "That can happen. I never had anything against him personally. It was Sam I never liked at any time." He ate for a few minutes, then put his knife and fork down. "Charlie, did Dal ever change his story about the Stiles shooting? He was there, saw it."

"I never asked him. And I don't think I will. He broke a lifetime habit. A man can go just so far against his own brother, Fields."

"I guess that's so."

There was a disturbance in the street and it drew Carlyle's attention briefly, then he went on eating; the clerk went out to see what it was all about, then came rushing into the dining room.

"Mr. Gunnison, you'd better come outside. Big Sam's got Dal down and is beatin' the hell out of him." He glanced at Gunnison's wife. "Beg your pardon, ma'am."

"You stay here," Gunnison said, touching his wife; he and Carlyle went outside and McKitrick and Pony Deal followed them.

There was a crowd blocking the street and the shouting was a din, a rush of excited sound with no particular meaning. Gunnison began pushing his way through the crowd, using his hands and elbows until he stood at the inner edge. He could see Gator and some of the Skillet men across the circle; Gator was standing motionless because Dannon was behind him and Gunnison suspected that the muzzle of Dannon's gun was nudged against Gator's kidney.

Dale Rainsford was in the mud, moving, but barely, and Big Sam staggered toward him, waving what was left of a sidewalk board; he had broken it against Dal and was now lifting it again.

"Don't do it," Gunnison said; he spoke loudly and it stopped Big Sam and he looked around to pinpoint the voice, then saw Gunnison.

He laughed and smashed the board down across Dal's

back, then threw the piece away. "I was through anyway, Charlie. You can have him now."

Gunnison stood there and then he saw Joel McKitrick moving through the crowd; he stepped behind George Dannon and quickly brought the barrel of his pistol down across Dannon's head. The man wilted and Gator stepped aside so he could fall and Big Sam saw it and knew that it meant trouble.

He started to turn, to push his way through the crowd, and he bumped into Carlyle and Pony Deal; they shoved him back and he stood there, looking first one way and then the other. "What the hell is this?" he asked. "I'm tired of this and I'm leaving."

"You're not going anywhere," McKitrick said flatly. "Take a look at the kid, Charlie."

Gunnison helped Dal Rainsford to a sitting position and tried to wipe some of the mud off his face. Rainsford's scalp was cut and bleeding and he supported him, half carried him to the watering trough where Rainsford simply submerged himself. He did this twice, then stood up under his own power and shook his head to clear it.

"What happened?" Gunnison asked.

Dal Rainsford looked at him, then said, "I want my chance now. The same kind of chance he gave me."

"You've got it," Carlyle said clearly.

Rainsford stepped out of the watering trough and took off his pants belt and tightly wound it around his fist, leaving eighteen inches and the big brass buckle dangling free. Big Sam looked at it and said, "What are you doin' to do? Hold me while he works me over?" He swung his head to the crowd. "Ain't anyone goin' to stop this?"

"What the hell for?" an unidentified man said. "He was walkin' along the street when you clouted him with the board. He never got a chance to set himself."

Gunnison said, "Is that right, Sam?"

"Well, hell, he's sneaky when he fights."

"There's been enough talk," McKitrick said. "He's all yours, kid."

"And I like that," Dal said and stepped toward his brother, his boots sucking at the mud in the street. Big Sam started to back up but McKitrick put out his foot, caught him in the buttocks, and shoved him forward and Sam went into Dal's swing. He yelled and clasped both hands to his head where the belt buckle had caromed off, taking hide and hair with it, and Dal kept his distance, hitting him again and again, across the hands, on the shoulders, hurting him, cutting him badly.

Big Sam was wailing and dancing, blood running down his face and off his hands and then Dal threw the belt away and doubled his fists. He came up to Sam with caution, yet determination, and he hit Sam flush in the mouth, driving him back a step. It set the big man to a fury and he rushed in, which was what Dal wanted, for he danced back and cut Sam over the eyes, then circled him, his fists cocked.

The rage took Big Sam completely over and he was an animal going on blind instinct, rushing, wasting himself, falling, getting up, cursing, and Dal was punishing him, whittling on him like a man working on a piece of pine with a penknife.

He had both of Sam's eyes completely closed and the man's lips were split and dripping blood, then Dal stood back while Sam charged around, stumbling, swinging at nothing, and when Sam ran into the hitchrail and fell over it, Dal Rainsford turned away.

The crowd was silent and Fields Carlyle said, "Well, don't you have homes?"

It broke them because it was a hard push, what they needed, and the crowd rapidly thinned. Big Sam was groping around in the mud and Gunnison walked over to where George Dannon lay; the man was stirring, moaning, trying to get up.

"He'll be all right," Gunnison said, and turned to go back to the hotel. As he reached the boardwalk he stopped and waited for Carlyle and the others to come up.

Gator said, "I'll look after the kid. He took some real licks."

After he trotted away, Carlyle said, "What started it?"

"Meanness," Gunnison told him. "Sam made a real mistake tonight." He turned and looked up and down the street. "Don't Dannon and Burdett have an office around here somewhere?"

"Next to the bank," McKitrick said.

"Let's go look at it," Gunnison suggested, and led the way.

There was lamplight coming through the windows and Gunnison opened the front door and stepped inside. Burdett was in the back room and he said, "Well, George, how did it go?"

When he got no immediate answer he looked out and saw them standing there and his smile faded.

"Expecting someone else?" Gunnison asked.

"I thought it was George," Burdett said.

"George has a headache," McKitrick said. "I hit him with my gun."

Burdett licked his lips, then sat down beside a rolltop. He shuffled some papers, then said, "Well, it don't mean anything to me. A man's got to look out for himself. If you had a quarrel with George, then it's between the two of you."

"There was some excitement out on the street," Carlyle said matter of factly. "Didn't you hear it, Kyle?"

"Well, I did hear something," Burdett said. "But I paid no attention to it."

"You ought to look into these things," McKitrick said. "Big Sam just got the livin' hell beat out of him."

"I thought he—" Burdett closed his lips tightly.

"Nothing's working out for you," Gunnison said dryly. "You ought to take the hint, friend, and back out."

"How can I?"

"It's something you'd better figure out," Gunnison told him, and they left.

Burdett sat there until he was sure they were well down the street, then he got up and went out and walked to the alley and carefully made his way down the muddy length to the back stairs of the hotel. He paused for a look at the top landing, then went down the dimly-lighted hall to a door and opened it.

Lana Rainsford was in her shift, sitting at the dresser, combing her hair. She looked at him through the mirror, then said, "It didn't work, did it?"

"Damn it, George said he could handle it. If Gunnison—"

"Is that all you can say?" She put the comb down and got up and faced him. "Haven't you any guts at all?"

"I can do what has to be done, when the time comes," Burdett said. "And I won't get myself killed doing it either." He heard a sound on the step and opened the door just as George Dannon put out his hand. "Come in. You've got a knot on your head."

Dannon hit him on the mouth for saying that, then walked over to the washstand, wet a towel and put it against his head. Lana watched him a moment, then Dannon said, "I didn't see anyone sneak up on me. Sam's a mess, huh?"

"You didn't scare anyone tonight," she said. "Isn't that what you were going to do, George, scare the hell out of Dal?"

"All right, all right," he said. "So it didn't come off."

"I've got a feeling that a lot of things aren't going to come off," she said. "Look at Kyle. He's ready to pack up and go home right now."

"It ain't that. It's just that the time's not right. We moved too fast."

"You move when I tell you to move," Lana pointed out.

"No woman bosses me," Burdett said.

She looked at Dannon. "You tell him, George."

"Aw, now let's not be that way."

"What is this?" Burdett asked. "What's the matter, George?"

"Let's not start fighting among ourselves," Dannon said. "And will you cut it out, Lana?" He jammed his hands into his pockets and glanced at Burdett. "There's something to what she says, Kyle. Why don't you go along, as a favor to me."

"What do I owe you?"

"As a favor." He looked at Burdett and saw that the man was not at all satisfied.

Then Lana Rainsford laughed and said, "George knows that I've had enough and will tell his wife what's been going on unless he comes into line. Isn't that right, George?"

Burdett swore softly. "Damn it, I should have known you was mixed up with her that way." He sat down and frowned and blew out a long breath. "I guess you want to run it all."

"Why shouldn't I? Do I make as many stupid mistakes as you two?"

14

Gator went over to Doctor Quinn's house and found Dal Rainsford sitting in Quinn's waiting room, a bandage around his head, and a livid bruise on his cheekbone. Dal was trying to roll a cigaret, but his arm had been lamed and he was having a tough time of it. Gator sat down, took the tobacco and paper and rolled the smoke, then gave it to Rainsford to lick and light.

"That's the first thing you ever did for me," Dal said.

"First time you deserved it," Gator said. "Big Sam in there?"

Dal nodded and drew on his smoke.

"He's bent up, huh?" Gator said.

"Some," Dal admitted. "I never enjoyed anything so much. All my life I've been takin' his licks. That's over now."

"He knows it, too," Gator opined. "You want to say anything about what happened at the fence that day?"

Young Rainsford shook his head. "I don't want to be the one who hangs him, Gator. God knows he's on a slide to hell, but do I have to give him the push?" He drew long on his smoke, then crushed the butt out in a potted plant that was on a nearby table. "Gunnison wouldn't fool around about it and you know it; he'd haul Sam off to jail." He looked at the dark dourness of the Frenchman's face. "I don't think you owe me anything, Gator. Surely no favors. But I'd appreciate not bein' pushed about this."

"I won't say anything," Gator said.

Doctor Quinn came out. He said, "I've had a busy night. And both men can afford to pay their bill, a rarity, I assure you." He lit his pipe and stood there, hands in his pockets. "Are you going to meet the train?"

"What train?" Gator asked.

Quinn frowned. "Didn't you know? I thought that's why everyone was in town. The Texas Development Company chartered a special train. It's due in around ten o'clock."

Dal Rainsford stood up. "I'll see you later, doc. Comin', Gator?"

"Sure, there's nothin' wrong with me."

Gunnison and Carlyle were at the hotel and when Rainsford came up he could see that Gunnison had heard about the train; they cut off their talk and looked at young Rainsford and Carlyle said, "How's your—" and he let it go when Dal waved his hand.

"We were talkin' about the train," Gunnison said. "You know about it?"

"Doc told us," Dal said. "They didn't waste any time, did they?"

"It's a special down from Cheyenne," Gunnison said. "And if my guess is worth a dime they're all raw-hiders, men who've been run out of a dozen counties already by big cattlemen. They're the kind Dannon would want to bring in, men with a built-in hate, men who'd fight a cattleman just because he was a cattleman. It made me wonder why they'd want to bring in farmers; they only want to plow and plant." He shook his head. "Fields, what do you want to bet we see some old familiar faces tonight?"

"I wouldn't bet that I don't," Carlyle said. "But I'm not in this, Charlie. Understand that now."

"You're goin' to wait until it's too late," Gunnison said. "Are you goin' to the depot with me?"

"I'll go that far," Carlyle said. "I guess the whole town will be there."

They left the hotel, buttoning their coats as they crossed the muddy street and walked to the depot. Melted snow left puddles of slush and there was a good-sized crowd trampling it. The cinder platform was crowded and they saw Dannon and Burdett there, and then Hank Freeman sidled up to them and spoke softly.

"I hope you're not goin' to make any trouble, Charlie."

"Now why would I do that?" Gunnison asked wryly. "They've only come here to cut up Skillet range with their fences and to rustle our cattle."

"Farmers ain't all like that," Freeman said.

"Wait'll you see these farmers."

They heard the train and finally caught the bright cell of the headlight, then an excitement seemed to catch up the crowd as the train pulled in, and Dannon and Burdett went forward, and as the train unloaded its passengers they lined them up on the platform and started to call off their names.

"Let's go," Gunnison said, but he didn't mean back to the hotel, and it took Gator and Dal Rainsford by surprise, the way he pushed through the crowd.

When Dannon saw him he closed his mouth and stood there. Gunnison took off his hat so that the lamplight cast no shadows on his face; they saw him and many of them knew him.

He singled a bearded man out and stepped up to him. "Moss Tedder," Gunnison said. "And your boys, Bub and Andy." He reached out quickly and tore open the man's coat at the throat, exposing ugly rope burns. "That's how close this man came to being hung for cattle rustling in Montana four years ago."

Moss Tedder grinned. "When I was told you was here, I couldn't wait to get here, Gunnison."

"You may not be here long," Gunnison said and moved along. He stopped in front of a stout man who had a wife and two gangly sons and a daughter with him. "What's your name?"

"Simmons," the man said. "This is my family."

He looked at Simmons' face, at his clothes, at his wife and kids, then said, "Why are you here?"

"For the land. When we got to Wyoming a month ago we couldn't find anything that suited us. We heard about this land and got on the train."

"Where's your gear?"

Simmons jerked his thumb toward a freight car. "Implements and wagon's in there. Livestock in the cattle car. You ask a lot of questions, mister."

"He's got no right," Dannon said.

Gunnison looked at him. "Then step out here and stop me, George." He turned his attention back to Simmons. "And I'm the man whose land you're going to roost on. What are you going to do with the land?"

"Raise grain," Simmons said. "I've got seed."

Gunnison singled Dal Rainsford out with his eyes. "You see that these people get some help in building a place. You see that they get on a creek where there's good water."

"See here," Dannon said. "I'll parcel out land to whom I please and you've—" He stopped talking when Gator jabbed an elbow into his ribs.

"Don't your head hurt enough for one night?" Gator asked.

Dannon scowled but shut his mouth and Charlie Gunnison walked on down the line. The next man grinned and chewed his tobacco and when Gunnison stopped, the man said, "I just knew I'd see you again, SixGun."

"Roan Banner? Jail's changed you some."

"It's made me hate more," Banner said. "Six years of it, Charlie. We're goin' to have a time, you and I."

"Make sure Dannon saves you a cemetery plot," Gunnison said and moved on.

He found old enemies there, men who had bumped heads with big cattlemen before and had lost. And he found families there who knew nothing at all about this, six of them farmers, not fighters, and to each of them he promised good land with water, and all the help Skillet could offer them.

They didn't understand it, and they didn't believe it, but they would in time. To the others he promised nothing because they knew him from Wyoming and Montana and he knew them, knew what they had come for.

He pushed back through the crowd and Carlyle joined him, and before they walked away from the station, Hank Freeman caught up with them.

"How about a drink at The Best Place?" Freeman asked.

They went there and he got a bottle and glasses and they sat around a table while he poured. "I was surprised," Freeman said. "Some of those families are nothin' but raw-hiders. I didn't think Dannon would bring that kind in. They won't be easy to handle."

"He's just goin' to turn 'em loose," Gator said. "Our fences will be cut soon enough."

Gunnison said, "Fields, you'd better look after your horses. Roan Banner's got an eye for good saddle stock. He beat a horse-stealing charge three years ago in Montana." He stopped talking when Freeman tapped him on the arm and he looked around as Judge Caldwell came in with Harry Wilson from the bank. They saw Gunnison at the table and came over and pulled up chairs without waiting for an invitation.

Caldwell said, "Harry came over and woke me. Gunnison, what kind of people came in on that train? He says there are toughs—"

Gunnison laughed and the judge stared at him, a little offended, and not seeing the joke at all. Harry Wilson said, "As leading citizens we're taking this very seriously, Gunnison."

"Don't you think I am?" Gunnison asked. "Have a drink. It'll calm you down."

"Damn it, I'm not excited. Freeman, where were you tonight?"

"At the depot."

"Aren't these men wanted for something?"

"Not that I know of," Freeman said. "But you give 'em time, Mr. Wilson, and they will be." He pushed his whiskey glass aside and leaned forward. "I've been poking along as a part-time deputy sheriff who had to tend bar to make a living. Now I suggest that you get your leading citizen influence down to the telegraph office and send a wire to the county seat, getting me appointed as a full-time deputy because in the next few months you're going to need a lawman who's not busy tending bar."

"Why—" Wilson began, then sat and looked at Freeman. "Yes, I think that had better be done. Come along, Jonathan." He got up. "Mr. Gunnison, trouble would upset everything, you know." He put on his gloves. "Old Man Rainsford brought peace to the community. We're used to it now. I don't think many of us know how to handle trouble."

"That could be why I came all the way from Wyoming," Gunnison said. "Because he knew that most of your spines had melted."

They frowned and turned and started out and were almost bowled over when Moss Tedder and his two sons bulled their way inside. They were followed by Roan Banner and the Deacon family, seven wild men led by a gaunt, wild-eyed father.

These men pushed their way to the bar and cleared a space for themselves and stood there drinking and laughing, then they turned around and had their look. Roan Banner saw Gunnison first and his smile faded in his eyes. He nudged Otey Deacon and Moss Tedder and they grew quiet.

Roan Banner said, "Ain't this a small world?" He counted by pointing. "Five of you. There's eleven of us." He looked at Tedder and the Deacons. "Did you ever figure, in a case like this, just how many of them we could get with the first volley?"

"I never did," Moss Tedder admitted. "But it's interestin', just thinkin' about it."

"While you're at it," Carlyle said dryly, "you'd better figure how many we'd get. Your coats are buttoned. Ours are open, so we'd get into action quicker. Your hands are cold and stiff because you just came from outside. Ours are warm 'cause we've been sittin' here a spell. So go ahead and start something."

"We was just talkin'," Banner said.

"Shut your mouth," Freeman advised.

They hadn't paid any attention to him until then. Deacon said, "That advice or are you tellin' us?"

"Tellin' you," Freeman said. "You got objections?"

"They want trouble," Carlyle said softly. "Tell you what, Charlie, I'll take that one on the end, the one with the beard. That'll be my first shot. Why don't you take the one with the big mouth?"

"All right," Gunnison said. "Which one do you want, Dal?"

He pointed. "The third from the right; I don't like his face right off. I'll do him in first." He looked at Gator. "Why don't you shoot the one in the buffalo coat?"

"Glad to. And the one next to him," Gator said. "He looks like he's long overdue for dyin' anyway."

"He does for a fact," Freeman said. "Why don't I take old man Deacon?"

"His name's Otey," Gunnison said. "O-T-E-Y. I mention that 'cause we want it spelled right on his tombstone."

"Comes to second choice," Fields Carlyle said dryly, "I'll shoot that young one next to Moss Tedder. You got a name, son?"

"They call him Bub," Gunnison said. "You want to give the signal to go, Fields?"

"Naw, you go ahead," Carlyle said. "I'll just go along when the shootin' starts."

Roan Banner wasn't smiling. He licked his lips and said, "Now just a damned minute—"

"We came in here for a drink," Moss Tedder said.

"You've had it," Freeman said. "Now get out."

"You're always tellin' people what to do, ain't you?" Otey Deacon said. He put his hands up to the buttons of his coat.

"Why don't I just toss the bottle up over my head so it lands behind us," Gator said. "When it hits, we'll go at it."

"That's a good idea," Carlyle said. "Anytime you're ready, Gator."

He put his hand around the neck of the bottle and there was a rush away from the men standing at the bar, then it was very quiet. Moss Tedder shrugged and said, "I've got to hunt a place to stay. Come on, Bub, Andy."

He turned and walked out and Otey Deacon motioned for his tribe to do the same. Roan Banner was alone for almost ten seconds, then he wheeled and slammed out and a sigh seemed to come into the room, and talk started, softly at first, picking up in volume.

The bar did a brisk trade as though the excitement had dried their throats. Carlyle poured one for himself, then said, "I was in a bit of a bind there, Charlie. You see, I left my gun in the hotel room but I couldn't exactly say that, now could I?"

Freeman stared at him, then blew out a long breath.

"I'm not carrying one," Dal said. "Looks like we were in the same boat, Fields." He turned his head and looked at Gator. "You got yours? I noticed you didn't have one when Sam jumped me."

Gator opened his coat and he wore no cartridge belt.

"Now just a minute," Freeman said. "You mean Charlie and I were—aw, come on now."

Gunnison laughed softly. "Hank, you're a nervy cuss. You were holding it alone. I took my gun off before having dinner with my wife."

"Give me that bottle," Freeman said and drank from it; he put it down and wiped tears from his eyes. "You know, if they'd called that bluff, I'd have looked pretty stupid, doin' all the shooting."

"I think," Carlyle said evenly, "we'd have beat you in that respect because I've never looked good jumping under a table." He looked from man to man and they all laughed.

"When you started it," Dal Rainsford said, "there wasn't anything I could do but go along. You, Gator?"

"At a time like that a man just keeps talkin' and hopin'. But I do think we ought to be shod from now on. They looked like they was rubbed a little raw when they went out."

"There's going to be another time," Charlie Gunnison said. "Let's have one more drink and call it a night."

15

George Dannon moved to town when the snow was gone and took rooms at the hotel; he told his wife that it made it easier to tend his business, and neglected to tell her it was closer to Lana Rainsford.

Dannon wasn't happy and when Kyle Burdett came into town that Saturday night, they met in Dannon's room and talked about it, and Dannon paced back and forth, trailing cigar smoke. "I expected it to move faster, Kyle. Damn it, Gunnison and his bunch ran a bluff in the saloon. Tedder and the others should have called him. It's what they're paid for."

"If you'd been there, what would you have done?" Burdett asked.

Dannon made a cutting motion with his hand. "Damn it, it was their job. We've got to stay clear of it or it won't look good later."

"When I meet something I can't handle alone, I get help or run," Burdett said. "You know, those farmers are makin' out all right. Skillet is helping them out. I didn't think Gunnison would do that."

"Who knows what that sonofabitch is going to do?" Dannon snubbed out his cigar. "We've got to get something going, Kyle. Gunnison gets stronger and we just sit here."

Burdett shrugged his shoulders. "Then do something. Me, I'm going to get a drink, load the wagon and go home."

"You're no help."

"I put up my money. You said you'd do the rest." He got up and turned to the door.

Dannon said, "If you see Sam, send him up."

"Now there's a nice guy," Burdett commented and went out.

He found Sam in front of one of Sintown's saloons and told him what Dannon had said and Sam Rainsford walked to the hotel and went up the stairs.

He found Dannon sitting by the window, looking at the main street and Dannon spoke without turning his head. "Do you like to make trouble, Sam?"

"It's the most interestin'," Rainsford admitted.

"Why don't you ride out to the Tedder place tonight and see what you can come up with?"

"Good idea. I'm not doin' anything tonight."

Dannon looked at him then. "Sam, whatever you do, do it good."

"If I ever started somethin'," Sam said, "there's no tellin' where I'd stop."

"Who asked you to?"

Sam laughed. "I guess I'll go out to the Tedder place now. You'll hear about it, George."

"Not until afterward," Dannon said. "And Sam, if you get in trouble, I don't even know you."

"I already figured that," Sam said and went out.

He had his horse in the small stable behind the hotel and went there, saddled up, and rode out of town. The Tedder clan was living in a soddy near a small creek that split Skillet pasture land, and not far to the west, Roan Banner had his solitary camp. West a piece, beyond Banner, Deacon and his boy, Otey, lived in a dugout.

When Sam approached the Tedder place, they bristled rifles until they recognized him, then Moss Tedder said, "Light a spell, Sam."

Rainsford dismounted and looked around. "You ain't been doin' much."

"Been waitin'," Moss Tedder said. "You got somethin' in mind?"

"I thought we could do something," Sam said. "We'd need Deacon and Banner."

Tedder chewed his tobacco a moment, then spoke without

turning his head. "Bub, you go fetch 'em. Andy, stir a fire and make some coffee."

Sam squatted and pulled his hat low over his eyes. "Any of the Skillet riders been around?"

"Not close enough to shoot at," Tedder admitted. "Is it so, what I heard, that Gunnison and Carlyle and the rest ran a bluff on us?" Sam nodded and Tedder's eyes turned hard. "That don't set too well with me." He chewed his tobacco and watched his son make coffee, then they had a cup. "We goin' someplace tonight?"

"It's Saturday," Sam said. "For a fact I know that Gunnison and bunch is comin' to town."

"How do you know?"

"At the store, on the loadin' platform in the alley there's about two wagon loads of stuff, all marked: Skillet. Gunnison will be in and he'll bring half the crew anyway. Maybe more."

"Ah," Tedder said. "Now I know where we're goin' tonight. I take it though that we're goin' to do more than shoot out a few windows."

"You take it right," Sam said.

Moss Tedder sipped his coffee and squinted. "Tell you somethin', Sam: If I had good sense I'd take my boys and light out of here. I ain't here 'cause I'm right and Gunnison's wrong. I've been on the outs of things all my life. Born to it, I guess. It's hard for some men to amount to anything; for me it's been a real effort. Stealin' comes natural to me; it's easier than work. I'd as soon tell a man a lie as the truth. But I'll tell you one thing, Sam, I just can't get over a thing, forgive anybody for anythin'. I guess that's why I'm here, 'cause I can't turn down another crack at Gunnison."

Bud Tedder came back with Roan Banner; they put up their horses and helped themselves to the coffee. "Deacon and Otey will be along, Pa," Bob said.

"There's a pair," Moss Tedder commented. "If I had a son like that I'd drown him."

"You got a couple of pips as it is," Banner said. "What's up?"

"A little action tonight," Sam said. "Most of Skillet will be in town."

"I wouldn't want to bother with it unless we burned the place to the ground," Banner said frankly. "If a man's going to come after me, I want him to have a good reason for it."

"We'll wait until it gets dark," Sam said.

Banner looked at him. "Why?"

Sam stared. "Well, it just seems the thing to do, that's all."

"If we went now, we'd be there by dusk," Banner said. "I'm for that."

Sam cleared his throat. "I thought I was running this."

Tedder turned his head and stared. "You just thought that, Sam. What do you want to do, Roan?"

"Burn him to the ground. He did that to me once."

Deacon scratched his whiskered face. "If anyone got in the way, it wouldn't hurt to shoot 'em, would it?"

"What else could you do?" Banner asked. He got up and threw the rest of his coffee away. "Let's go." He kicked out with his foot and rapped Sam Rainsford on the shin. "You too."

"At night they wouldn't see us," Sam said.

Deacon laughed. "That what you're afraid of, them seein' you? Hell, I could smell you, Sam. I didn't have to see you to know what you was."

They got their horses and weapons and Tedder went to his wagon for a two gallon tin of coal oil, then mounted up. Sam would have been happy to tag along at the rear, but Otey Deacon gouged him in the ribs with his rifle and made him ride ahead of him, near the front.

They rode through open, rolling range, crossing a nearly dry creek and finally cresting a small rise. The main ranch buildings were visible in the distance, bright in the last rays of the sun. Banner guessed the distance at two miles and turned and looked at the last of the sun. He said, "Just about right. Thirty or forty minutes." He turned in the saddle and spoke to Deacon. "You and your boy hit the bunkhouse. If he's got a light crew there you ought to be able to take care of it."

"We can take care of it," Deacon said.

Betty Gunnison had every intention of going to town; at least earlier in the day that had been her intention, but the spring-warm day had made the baby fretful, so she decided to stay at the ranch with Letty Shannon and the two Mexican servants.

The crew had gone in with the wagons, except Shag and the cook, and she was looking forward to evening with its cooling breeze; the baby would sleep and she could sit on the porch and wait for her husband to come home.

The cook and his helper were scrubbing the floor of the cookshack and Shag came out of the bunkhouse, stood a moment by the door, looking off, then went back inside. He was gone only a moment when he reappeared, his cartridge belt and pistol around his hips, and carrying his rifle. Quickly he trotted across the yard and came to the porch.

"Riders coming," he said, pointing.

Both Letty and Gunnison's wife got up and walked to the end of the porch and looked. Letty said, "That's Big Sam; I know his horse."

"We've got trouble," Shag said softly. "They wouldn't be here if they didn't know the crew was gone." He turned to Letty. "What kind of guns are in the house?"

"There's a rack of rifles and plenty of ammunition."

"Let's break 'em out," Shag said and went on inside.

The guns were in Gunnison's office; he got the keys from the desk and opened the rack, handing repeaters and boxes of ammunition to Gunnison's wife and Letty Shannon.

"Get the baby and get on the top floor," he said. "Letty, you take the back of the house. Mrs. Gunnison, you call the servants."

He ran out and called the cook and his helper; by the time they reached the house, the servants appeared and Shag gave the orders and no one argued with him. He gave the two Mexicans each a rifle and two boxes of shells and sent them upstairs to cover both sides of the house.

"What do you want me to do?" Betty Gunnison asked. "I can shoot as straight as most men."

"Put the baby where she'll be safe, then stay with Letty," Shag said. "We'll stay down here and cover the yard."

"You be careful now," Betty said and went up the wide stairs.

The cook was a toothless man with a shining, hairless head, and an eagerness to fight in his eyes. He said, "That window looks good to me over there." He put a square box of cartridges in his hip pocket and went over, sitting down so he could peer over the sill.

The cook's helper, a gangly young man still in his teens, went to the other side and waited there; Shag stood near the open front door, but back so that he was out of sight.

They waited for what seemed a long time, then he heard the sound of horses coming on slowly. The light was fading; it wouldn't last another twenty minutes, then he saw Deacon and his son move toward the cookshack and the bunkhouse.

The others stayed in the yard, alert, weapons in hand, while Deacon and his boy got down. Deacon went into the cookshack while the boy went inside the bunkhouse and they could hear them ramming around. Otey came out and said, "Nobody here, Roan."

"Fire it then," Banner said and the boy took the can of coal oil from Tedder. He took two long strides toward the bunkhouse and Shag shouldered his .40-82 Winchester and shot him through. The boy tumbled in a loose rolling sprawl and for an instant the mounted men sat there, stunned, then they went off their horses and ran for cover.

Old Man Deacon started to run toward his boy, but the cook fired and hit him in the leg and Deacon dragged himself to a parked wagon and took cover there.

Someone ran around to the side of the house and there was rifle fire from an upstairs window and then it broke off. Tedder and his boys were by the corral and Big Sam took refuge behind the well curbing.

Roan Banner's voice boomed. "Hold your damned shootin'! It'll be dark soon."

"I told you to wait!" Sam yelled.

"Shut your fool mouth," Banner advised. "Deacon, you hurt bad?"

"I'll live," Deacon said. "My boy's dead though."

"Somebody had to get killed," Banner said. "Be glad it wasn't you."

Shag, crouched by the door, looked at the yard, placing them well in his mind. Darkness would make things a bit tougher, but it would work both ways, providing cover and yet hindering them if they tried to storm the house.

There was no doubt in Shag's mind that they intended to do this, and he waited, not intending to throw away ammunition; there would be plenty of shooting later.

Deep shadows grew in the yard as the light faded, then he saw one of Tedder's boys dash for the fallen coal oil can. Shag fired and drew a return volley that made him pull his head down. Bullets shattered the windows and thudded into the walls, and as he crouched there, he saw the reflected brightness of the mounting fire and raised up to see the bunkhouse going up, the dry planks fed by the coal oil.

The Tedder boy was soaking the cookshack and the firelight made a good target of him. As Shag shouldered his rifle, he could hear Moss Tedder yelling at his boy, then Shag squeezed off and watched the Tedder boy fall into the fire he had set.

Instantly, from the vicinity of the well and the corral came an answering fire and Shag started to pull back, then spun as a bullet caught him high in the chest. He fell in the doorway and tried to drag himself to cover, but he didn't have the strength.

He could see the whole yard, bright now with firelight, and he knew they could see him; he tried to pull his rifle around for one more shot, but he couldn't do it. So he put his head down and waited and he heard Old Man Deacon yell: "Let me! Let me!"

He heard the shot and the bullet made him jump, then a

roaring filled his mind, a sound like tumbling rocks, and he remembered nothing else.

The cook looked at him, and the cook's helper said, "Be he dead, Jake?"

"I guess he be. Better hike up and tell the wimmen about it."

The boy nodded. "We gettin' out of here, Jake?"

"We'll go when I say," Jake said softly.

"Anyway, he got two of 'em, didn't he, Jake?"

"He did, but I consider it no trade. The whole passle of 'em wasn't worth one of Shag."

"I'll go tell the women," the boy said.

"Tell 'em to come down here," Jake said. "If they do fire the house, I don't want 'em trapped upstairs."

"All right," the boy said, and left.

16

There were no lights on in the house and Betty Gunnison gathered them in the hallway, the large open foyer that had to be crossed to get into the house. There was a back door and several side doors, but to enter the house they would have to come through the kitchen or the library and into the foyer.

She put the baby in the bottom drawer of an oak highboy and stood there, rifle in hand. To the cook's helper, she said, "What's your name?"

"Mulberry, ma'am."

"Do you think you can sneak out, get a horse out of the south corral, and get to town without being caught?"

"I guess I can," he admitted.

"Then use the back door and be careful. We'll do our best to hold them off from the house until you get back."

"I'll hurry," he said and scooted out.

She turned to the two Mexicans. "If you stay here, you'll just get killed. Jake, take them with you and—"

"Me? I ain't goin' anywhere," Jake said. "They can go if they want, but I'm stayin'. I've been here forty years. Where'd I go?"

From the yard, Roan Banner yelled: "Hey, the house! Let's have a talk!"

"Don't anyone answer him," Betty Gunnison said. "That fire will attract the farmers. They'll come here and see what's the matter."

"And get themselves killed," Jake said. "Sam and his friends are gonna make a clean sweep of it, now that they got the chance."

"I'm afraid you're right," Betty said. "There's Tedder and one of his boys left, and Banner, Deacon, and Sam. Five. If they decided to rush the house, or fire it, we wouldn't be able to stop them." She stood a moment, thinking, then said, "If we could get out without being seen—"

"Out the back we might make it," Letty Shannon said.

They all started, surprised, when a rifle went off in the doorway, then they saw Shag moving his legs and they rushed to him, pulled him back out of the way. There was blood on his thigh where a bullet had broken his leg, and another had hit him in the shoulder, ranging downward, but losing its force before it could strike a vital organ.

"Thought you was dead, Shag, boy," Jake said, lifting the boy's head.

"They still—out there?" Shag asked.

"Yes, they're there," Betty Gunnison said. "Get some blankets, Letty. We'll stay."

There was a sound at the rear of the house, then pans came clattering down in the kitchen and a man cursed loudly. The cookstove was dumped over and glass shattered, and through an open doorway they could see the bright flare of fire.

Then Bub Tedder bounded through the door and into the foyer, a pistol in each hand. Jake shot and nicked young

Tedder, spinning him around. He went down on one knee, firing his pistols fast.

Letty Shannon gasped and slowly eased herself to the floor, and Betty Gunnison shouldered her rifle calmly and shot Bub Tedder through the head. Levering her rifle, she caught Moss Tedder as he came after his son and the old man was flung back against the wall, his arms outstretched, then blood ran from his mouth and he fell on his face.

Jake said, "She's gone. Didn't suffer any."

Betty Gunnison looked at the girl and she wanted to cry and knew that it wasn't possible; there just wasn't time in war. She handed her rifle to Jake and went to the highboy and got the baby.

Sam Rainsford was running around the yard, yelling for Tedder and Banner, then Old Man Deacon brought up the horses and they mounted up and wasted no time getting out.

The house was going good and there would be no saving it.

Jake said, "It's goin' to get hot before the night's over. Near the well's the best place fer us."

The two Mexicans were given the job of carrying Shag, and they tore down the screen door for a litter. Betty said, "What about Letty, Jake?"

"She's dead. It's bad, ma'am, but we've got to care for ourselves."

They went out and crossed the yard to the well and stayed there while the barn and bunkhouse and all the outbuildings crashed down in a shower of sparks and the huge house towered a column of flame and smoke that could be seen for miles around.

Lyle Simmons was the first to arrive; he had his wagon and his family with blankets and food and pots and Betty Gunnison met him as he drove across the yard. Simmons stopped and looked at the fire and it frightened him and he made no attempt to hide it. Then he saw Tedder's boy, dead by the bunkhouse, charred, only vaguely recognizable as having been human once, and he said, "What a terrible thing. Terrible!"

"Mr. Simmons, we have a wounded man by the well. Would you drive your wagon over there and take him to town to the doctor?"

"Certainly, certainly," Simmons said and clucked to the team.

He stopped by the well and Jake helped Simmons' wife down. The oldest boy looked around, wide-eyed, then helped unload blankets from the wagon. Jake showed him how to make a litter, and a cradle of rope so that Shag would be comfortably suspended in the wagon and while they were doing this, Pearson and his two boys arrived, and a few minutes later Jellico and a family named Ridenhour showed up.

They all had wagons and what goods they could load in a hurry, and although it seemed foolish, with everything hot ashes, they built a fire by the well and cooked food and made coffee and it somehow took the tragedy away from all this.

Simmons' boy and Jake drove toward town with Shag in the wagon, and only then did anyone ask what had happened. Jellico put it into words. "Was it your house that went up, or one of the outbuildings, I'd say it was a natural thing. But there's a dead man over there, so I guess it ain't." He was a string of a man, near fifty, with a farmer's gravity.

"We were burned out," Betty Gunnison said. She looked at Jellico a moment, then turned away and put her face in her hands and cried.

Simmons' wife stayed with her and the baby, and the men stood around, not saying anything.

The sound of approaching horsemen alarmed them, but Betty said, "It's all right." She knew it wasn't Banner or Deacon coming back; there were at least a dozen horses, maybe more, coming on fast. Then she saw her husband and Dal Rainsford and Carlyle and the Skillet crew and some of Carlyle's men, riding into the yard, filling it, swinging off, crowding around.

Gunnison rushed up and put his arms around her, holding her for a moment, then he stepped back and said, "Mulberry found us; we were a mile this side of town. We met the wagon with Jake and Shag." He looked at Simmons and the others. "I'm grateful that you're here. I won't forget this."

"We wish we could have done more," Ridenhour said. "But they were gone when we got here. What can we do?" He took Gunnison by the arm. "We want to help."

Dal Rainsford said, "You do what you think you can, mister. Charlie, you asked me what happened at the fence when Stiles was killed. All right, I'll tell you. Sam shot him cold. Stiles never had a gun. He was bringin' back a calf that had strayed through to his place." He turned his head and looked around. "Letty? Where's Letty?"

"She's dead," Betty Gunnison said softly. "She was killed when we were trying to hold the house."

"Which one did it?" Carlyle asked.

"The Tedders. They're dead too. I killed them both."

"What are we hanging around here for?" Dal Rainsford said. "We've got things to do."

"It'll wait an hour or two," Gunnison said. "Gator, take the crew and look around. Save what you can. The tack shed looks scorched, but there'll be lanterns inside. Break out a few. Get some light around the well here. Take care of the stock."

The foreman nodded and stepped into the saddle and took the crew with him. Gunnison dipped into the well for the water bucket, filled it and passed it around. Dal Rainsford stood there, his expression dark. Then he blurted: "Charlie, if I was to leave now, would you stop me?"

"Yes," Gunnison said.

"In the name of hell, why?" he shouted.

"Because you're not thinking now. Just acting on instinct. It's no good, Dal. We'll gain more by waiting than we'll lose. First, we want to get the straight of it." He turned to his wife and put his arms around her. "Who got away?"

"Sam. And Deacon, but Shag hit him in the leg."

"His boy, Otey?"

"Shag killed him first shot. Then Andy Tedder."

"And Roan Banner got away?" Carlyle asked.

"Yes, three of them."

"Then we ought to be riding," Dal maintained.

Gunnison glanced at him. "Where'll Sam go? To town? We'll find Sam and when we do, I want him arrested, you understand? Arrested and tried for killing Stiles. Not shot on the spot." He thought a moment. "Banner didn't have much when he came here. And Deacon's got a bullet in him. We can bed down here and wait 'til daylight."

"That's damned good sense," Fields Carlyle said. "If we go rammin' around the country tonight some more are going to get killed. Deacon and Banner will shoot at shadows if they get a chance."

Gunnison was watching Dal Rainsford. "Let me say something and I want you to think about it. The old man died thinking that none of his kin was worth two whoops in hell, but right now it seems that there's some hope for you. Don't spoil it now by acting like a damned fool."

"Sam didn't think of this himself," Carlyle put in. "We'll get Sam, and Dannon and Burdett too. Do you see that, Dal?"

"I guess I do," he said, "but it's an effort."

Gunnison slapped him on the arm and said no more about it. Gator came across the yard with several lanterns and hung them by the well; they would make the night camp there and in the morning survey the damage and figure out where to start over.

Gunnison spent an hour inspecting the corrals and the stock; there was no damage there. Then Jake and his helper came back, each driving a loaded wagon; he swung down and said, "We left the other one parked behind the store. Leastways we'll eat."

He took a lantern and went to the tackshed and got gunnysacks and soaked them and tied them around his feet and walked around the hot ashes of the burned out cookshack, salvaging badly warped pots and pans. These were scrubbed thoroughly and a little after midnight he had a tasty cauldron of stew about ready to serve.

There was some stacked lumber in back of the corral that hadn't burned and they put up rough tables and ate in shifts.

Dal Rainsford sided up to Gunnison and said, "How are you going to tie this to George Dannon, Charlie?"

"Maybe we won't," Gunnison said, loading a tin plate with stew. "Even if Sam says he was put up to it, Dannon can say it's a lie. We'll see, Dal."

Young Rainsford filled a skillet lid and took it over to a place across from Gunnison and his wife. "Charlie, if I left my gun here, would you let me leave now?"

"What's on your mind?"

"An idea. Charlie, I give you my word I won't lift a hand against anyone."

Gunnison thought about it, then said, "Leave when you like."

Rainsford nodded and took off his gun. "I'll leave my rifle here too." He finished his stew, threw the lid in the washwater, then got his horse. After he mounted and rode out, Gator came over, the question in his eyes, and Gunnison said, "I told him he could leave."

Dal Rainsford didn't take the town road, but cut across the open range toward the Dannon place, and he raised the dark outline of the buildings in the small hours of the morning. A dog started barking and a man came out of the bunkhouse with a pistol and a lantern; he seemed surprised to see Rainsford.

"I want to see Mrs. Dannon," Dal said. "It's important."

"It had better be," the man said and led the way to the house. He called to her and she lighted a lamp and came to the door, a robe tightly wrapped around her.

She looked at Dal Rainsford and said, "What do you want here?"

"I came from town. Your husband needs you, ma'am. He said for me to drive you in."

"You're lying."

"Why would I do that?"

"You're no friend of his," she said. "He wouldn't send you."

"It's some trouble he's havin' with Burdett," Dal said. "Guess he couldn't trust anyone but me. We was never enemies, you know."

"If you're lying, George will skin you alive," she said. "I'll get dressed. Sims, hitch up a buggy."

The man went to the barn and Dal Rainsford waited by the porch, smoking and feeling pretty good about it so far. She took her time but finally came out and Sims brought the buggy from the barn and Rainsford tied his horse on behind and got in. He drove out and took the town road and for awhile she didn't say anything.

"Must get lonely out here with George in town so much," he said.

"He's a man who likes his way," she said flatly, and he knew that it was a sore spot with her and that she had brooded about it some.

He said, "I never did trust Burdett, you know, and I guess George has seen this coming for some time. Burdett wants to hog it all for himself."

"What kind of trouble was there?" she asked.

He hesitated, as though it was sad news and he didn't know how to tell her. She caught the whiff of trouble because she had a nose for it, fears of her own.

"There was shootin'?"

He started to speak, then closed his mouth and nodded. "He's hurt some. A man needs his woman then, I guess."

"Why the devil didn't you say so in the first place?" she snapped, and grabbed the reins with one hand and the whip with the other. She lashed the team into a run and he sat there and smiled inwardly; he had her going now, had her acting without thinking and he had to admit that Charlie Gunnison was right: when a person did that they were bound to do something stupid.

17

The town was dark and silent when they reached the end of the street and Dal Rainsford took the reins from Mrs. Dannon and slowed the horses to a walk. Farther down a gleam of lamplight brightened the hotel windows; the night clerk had a lamp lighted and Rainsford pulled up to the hitchrack and stopped.

He moved around the rig to help her down, but she didn't wait for him and he went on ahead of her; the lobby was empty except for the clerk who snored in a tilted back chair. She started over to wake him but Rainsford took her arm and shook his head and they went up the stairs together.

The upper hallway was dark and he stopped and took one of the lamps from the brackets, lifted the glass and put a match to the wick. Then he handed it to her and led the way down the hall, looking at the room numbers as they went along.

They passed one door and Mrs. Dannon said, "This is my—"

"Shhh," he said and moved on.

He stopped before a door, carefully tried the knob, and found it locked. Then he backed up and before she could protest, he lunged against the door, driving all his weight against it. The pine jamb splintered and the door crashed open and a woman yelled in surprise and a man cursed as he fumbled for his gun buried somewhere under his pants piled on a chair.

Mrs. Dannon raised the lamp so that it shined into the room and George Dannon sat up in bed, the hair on his chest and shoulders dark and thick. Lana Rainsford kept the covers pulled up around her throat and they stood that way, the woman with the lamp, and the two in bed.

Then Mrs. Dannon said, "George, you lyin' cheat, I'm goin' to kill you!"

"Now, Cora," he said and started to get out of bed. She put the lamp down and rushed for his clothes piled in the chair and kicked them to the floor as he tried to disentangle his legs from the blankets.

She grabbed his holstered pistol, but before she could pull it free, he was wrestling with her for it and she kicked and bit him, and he swore, but finally got the gun away from her. To keep her from having it he threw it out the open window to the street; Dal Rainsford heard it hit in the dust, then Cora Dannon stood there, looking at her husband, her breathing heavy and violent in the stillness of the room.

"So this is what you're going to do to me, George," she said. "I'm not goin' to let you."

"Cora, we can talk about this," Dannon pleaded. He tried to touch her but she jerked away and slapped at him.

"No we can't!" She turned to the door and stood there a moment. "I've took you all these years, good with the bad, but I won't stand for this, George. Sure, I ain't much and my looks is gone, but I'm not goin' to let you do this to me. You hear? When you come out, I'll be waitin' for you and I'll tell you this: no jury in the world will hang me for what I'm goin' to do."

He opened his mouth to plead with her but she turned and went down the hall and he dropped his hands lifelessly to his sides.

Dal Rainsford said, "She meant that George."

Dannon seemed to remember that he was there and looked at him. "Why?" he asked. "Will you tell me that?"

"I promised Charlie Gunnison I wouldn't kill you," Rainsford said. He took out his sack tobacco and made a cigaret. "Sam and his friends did a good job, George. Skillet is ashes, burned to the ground. Letty's dead."

"You can't blame that on me," Dannon said hotly.

Lana swore softly and got out of bed and she rushed over and hit Dannon in the face. "You damned fool! I wanted that house! What good is it ashes?"

He rudely pushed her back. "Get some clothes on, you cheap bitch," he snapped, then turned to pick up his clothes off the floor. He slipped into his pants. "You've got no right to think I had anything to do with it. No right at all. Just try and prove something."

"Not going to have to," Dal said mildly. "You know, I wouldn't turn on Sam, or you, Lana, because we were brother and sister. But it came to me sudden like that there wasn't anything else to do." He shook his head. "The Old Man was good, Lana. And somehow it always was in my mind that in you and Sam there must be something good too. But there ain't. Some people are just mean and no good and there's no accountin' for it." He looked steadily at George Dannon. "Moss Tedder is dead. So are his boys, Bub and Andy. Otey Deacon is dead and the old man's got a bullet in his leg. Come dawn, the country will be crawling with riders from Skillet and Carlyle's and every lawman in north Texas will be on the lookout for those three, together, or alone. So you see how it is, George? Gone boom, ain't it?"

Lana sat down on the edge of the bed and looked at her bare legs. "All I wanted was the money, Dal. Is that so wrong?"

"Don't you know?" He stepped to the door. "Go back to bed. Enjoy yourselves. What's left for you?"

He pulled the damaged door closed, but it wouldn't stay that way, swinging slightly ajar. The clerk was standing at the head of the stairs, a lamp and a pistol in hand, but he showed no intention of coming farther.

"Is everything all right?" he asked.

"Just fine," Rainsford said. He walked past, then stopped. "What made you ask?"

"The door crashed—" He stopped. "Are you sure? Mrs. Dannon's standing outside with a pistol in her hand."

"She's going to shoot her husband when he comes out. Nothing for you to worry about."

The clerk swallowed. "That's terrible! Does Hank Freeman know about this?"

"You ought to go tell him."

"She ought to be stopped," the clerk said flatly.

Rainsford put his hand on the man's shoulder. "Friend, let me tell you something. She's going to shoot her husband; her mind's made up. Now wouldn't it be better if she did it here, with witnesses, than someplace where it was her word only?" He patted the man and went on down the stairs and out to the street.

Cora Dannon was sitting in the buggy; she had picked up the pistol and was holding it in her hand. Rainsford stopped and she said, "I know how you could turn against your own kind, Dal. I know because I could turn against George. Do you know, I love him. That's why I can sit here and do what I'm goin' to do." She reached out and touched him. "That sister of yours, do you think she loves him too?"

"No," Dal said. "She won't cry over him."

The clerk came out, glanced at them and hurried on down the dark street. She said, "Where's he going?"

"After the deputy, I suppose," Dal said. "Freeman will take the gun away from you."

"Then I'll get another," she said simply. "If it ain't today, it's tomorrow. George knows me when I get my back up."

"You could let him say he was sorry and let it go at that."

"He wouldn't be sorry, not George." She sighed. "He'd say it though. He's lied enough now to make another easy for him." She looked up, at the window framed in lamplight and it stirred the anger in her mind and she lifted the gun and fired and watched the bullet make the curtain jump.

Then George Dannon stuck his head out and she used her whole hand to ear the hammer back and fired again, chipping wood from the frame near his head.

Boots pounded the walk and Hank Freeman came up, his shirt yet unbuttoned. He reached out and took the pistol from Cora's hand and said, "Now we can't have you shootin' in the middle of the night, can we?"

"I'll get another gun as soon as the store opens up," Cora said. "You know that, deputy?"

Freeman sighed and ran his fingers through his uncombed hair. "Mrs. Dannon, why don't you just let your husband go his own way? I guess it's too late to settle this any other way than with a lawyer. Wouldn't it be better that way?"

"What you got in mind?"

Her cooperation cheered Freeman; he said, "Let me go up to talk to George. Suppose I tell him to get out, catch the seven o'clock train? Then you could see a lawyer and do things nice and quiet now with no one really gettin' hurt?"

She looked at him oddly. "You think no one's been hurt already? All right, you go tell him that."

Freeman smiled and nodded and went inside.

Cora Dannon unwrapped the reins from around the whip. "I'll go back alone, if you don't mind."

"I'm going that way," Dal said. "I don't mind—"

"But *I* do," she said. "I need time alone."

"Yes," he said, "of course." He stepped back and she pulled the team around when he untied them and he watched her drive out.

George Dannon's swearing was loud and beneath it, cutting through it, was Hank Freeman's unbending determination. The clerk came out.

"All this trouble will give the place a bad name."

"When did it ever have a good one?" Dal asked.

Freeman came down and stopped on the walk. "Your sister wants to see you, Dal."

"What about?"

"She didn't say."

He hesitated, then went on up and met Dannon in the hallway. The man had a suitcase in his hand and when he saw Rainsford a pent up anger within him gave way and he threw the suitcase. Dal let it bounce off his shoulder by turning quickly and he hardly straightened when Dannon rushed him. He hit Rainsford a blow that sent him reeling against the wall and a man in the room yelled, "For God's sake, let's have some quiet!"

Dannon crowded Dal Rainsford, his hands going to the throat and Rainsford raised his knee and connected solidly with Dannon's crotch. The man's mouth flew open and his eyes looked like two blue eggs and the blood drained from his face as he sat down quickly, both hands covering himself. His expression remained unchanged and he rocked forward, unable to speak or cry out. Then he drew in a long breath and rolled over on his side, his knees drawn almost to his chin.

Rainsford said, "You're clumsy, George."

He went on down the hall then and opened the door of his sister's room and when he looked at the splintered casing he felt a little proud of himself. She was dressed now, throwing things into her suitcases.

"I want to know," she said, "just what made you think you were so holy."

"Did I say that?" He shrugged. "Lana, you know what the old man wanted of us? He wanted us to work for what we got. That's all. Just do some old-fashioned work."

She straightened and fastened some leather straps. "Dal, I need money."

"Was there ever a time when you didn't?"

"Look, this is no time to—" She stopped and softened her tone. "Well, Dal, will you do this last thing for me?"

He shook his head. "I've done my last thing for you. No money. Where would I get it?"

"You still have your two thousand."

"It's mine. I'm going to keep it. Are you going with George?"

"Do you expect me to stay around here now?" She set her suitcases on the floor. "Dal, let me have the money. I have to live, don't I? What will George have? His wife will take everything he owns through the courts."

"Lana, you sat in on the game and you lost. Quit crying about it."

"Sure. Sam will end up hanged and you'll have it all."

"I guess Sam was always meant to be hanged," he admitted. "But he had his choice just like the rest of us." He turned to the door. "Was there anything else, Lana?"

"You won't give me the money?"

He dug into his pocket and laid sixty dollars in gold on the dresser. "You can have that. And you keep in touch, Lana.

You let me know where you are and I'll send you some every month."

"You will? How much?"

"Fifty dollars," he said. "Just enough to keep you from havin' to walk the streets."

He went out. She threw something at him but he didn't look back, didn't care enough for that.

Freeman and the clerk were still outside, talking. George Dannon was across at the watering trough, washing his face. Freeman said, "What happened to him? He came out, all crouched over, threw up and staggered across the street."

"Upset stomach, I guess," Rainsford said.

The clerk went inside and he seemed gone no more than a minute; he came out and motioned for Rainsford to come to the door where Freeman wouldn't hear. "Say," he said, "did you take my derringer from behind the counter?"

"No."

"Think I ought to—"

"You keep your mouth shut," Dal said and crossed over to where his horse was standing to dropped reins. He swung up, then spoke to Freeman. "I'm going back. If Sam comes to town, you know what to do."

"I know," Freeman said and turned down the street.

Rainsford went behind the hotel, dismounted, and struck several matches. He saw the marks left by Cora Dannon's buggy, and he stood there and thought about this, trying to decide what to do. Then he made up his mind, stepped into the saddle and rode home.

Jules Gentry dealt in yard goods, notions, light farm implements, and just about anything else he could turn a profit on, and he was riding the northbound day coach after seven days on the road. When the train pulled into the station, Gentry took off his derby and looked through the grimy window. There was a tall, mustached man there, suitcases at his feet, but his eyes went to the woman, young, proud, pretty, and seemingly very angry. While he was watching her, he saw another woman step out of the depot and the man's head came around quickly and he put up both hands as though surprised.

Then the woman took a hand from behind her and pointed a derringer at the man; Gentry stared; the gun went off; he saw the puff of powder, saw the man raise a hand to his breast as though touched by heartburn; there was no sound for the coach was noisy and the window was closed.

The other woman put both hands over her mouth and the woman with the derringer fired again, as the man was falling, and when he hit the cinders he rolled so that Gentry could see the blood on his breast, and on his forehead where the second bullet had hit him.

He started to get up, to speak, but there was no sound in him, then the coach gave a lurch and the train pulled out of the station and it infuriated Genty, to have seen this, and to know nothing of it.

It was, he thought, a meaningless, bad dream. He turned to tell someone else, but they evidently had not seen it; they were talking and laughing and he sat weakly down and wiped the sweat from his face.

A moment later he took a bottle of whiskey from the bottom of his valise and drank deeply, then leaned back and closed his eyes.

18

Kyle Burdett woke before dawn. There was the smell of smoke in the wind and it alarmed him; he dressed and went outside and found his foreman and two of the crew standing in the yard.

Burdett said, "There's a fire somewhere."

"That's wood, not grass," the foreman said. He tested the gentle wind with a wet finger. "The wind's blowin' across Skillet range. You don't suppose—?"

"I'm not going to saddle up and ride over there to find out," Burdett said.

His wife came to the door. "Kyle, what you doin' up?"

"Go back to bed," he said. "It's no mind to you."

"It ain't no mind to you either, whatever it is," she snapped, and closed the door.

"Damned woman's got to poke her nose into everything," Burdett muttered. "Curly, come morning, why don't you have one of the men ride over for a look?"

The foreman looked at the sky; the darkness was already starting to thin in the east. "Another hour or so," he said, then stopped and cocked his head. "You hear that?"

Burdett had; he held up his hand and both men stood there, mouths open for silent breathing, heads cocked to one side. "Horses," Curly said. "Comin' on slow. Careful like."

"I make it three," Burdett said. He waved his hand at the two men standing a few feet away. "Get your guns. There's no tellin'."

The three men ran to the bunkhouse and Burdett hurried inside; he came back out with a rifle and waited on the porch. Visibility was growing slowly and through the dull gray he could see the three men come into his yard. When they were yet seventy yards away, he said, "Sing out there! Who the hell is it?"

"It's me, Big Sam."

"Who's with you?"

"Banner and Deacon," Sam said. "Deacon's been hurt."

"Then take him to town to the doctor," Burdett advised.

"We're comin' in," Sam said. "We need fresh horses."

"Like that, huh?" Burdett said. "Been up to somethin'?"

"Let us come in and talk about it," Sam suggested.

"You come in alone," Burdett said. "There's rifles on you, so mind what I say."

They held a conference, a brief one, then Sam rode on to the porch and Deacon and Banner started to ease their horses over toward the barn. A rifle slammed echoes over the yard and Banner's hat was whipped off his head and then

Curly said, "Move again and the next one will be six inches lower."

Sam stopped at the porch and when he started to swing down, Burdett said, "You can talk from there. What you been up to, Sam? No damned good, that's for sure."

"Kyle, you ought to help Deacon. He's got a bullet in his leg. You can't expect a man to get far hurt like that."

"You ain't answered me."

Sam fell silent for a moment, then he told Burdett what had happened and Burdett listened to it and when Sam was finished, Burdett pointed the rifle at Sam's chest. "You get the hell off my place right now or I'll shoot you dead."

"Wha—"

"You heard me. Git! Damn you, comin' here like this. Every Skillet rider will be lookin' for you three and if they find you here they'll think I was a part of it." He took a step toward Sam and Sam backed his horse. "Go on! Git the hell off! I'm not goin' to be killed for what you've done!"

From the yard, Roan Banner said, "Didn't I tell you, Sam?" He left the saddle in a dive, taking his rifle with him and it surprised everyone that he would make his fight there in the open.

Curly opened up from the bunkhouse, but he fired too quick and missed Banner.

From his saddle, Deacon raised his rifle and never got to fire it; a volley wiped him from the saddle and he fell like a wet sack of meal and his horse trotted away.

Banner swung his gun and killed the animal, then sprinted toward it amid a sprinkle of bullets and fell down behind it.

At the porch, Sam Rainsford threw his hands in the air and stepped off the horse at Burdett's invitation; he came close and was disarmed and made to sit with his head against the wall, hands high.

The shooting stopped; there was no sense wasting cartridges. Banner couldn't move from behind the dead horse and none of Burdett's men dared jump up and rush him.

They were like that when the sun came up.

Gunnison reached the Dannon place before dawn; he had sixteen Skillet riders, seven men from Fields Carlyle's place, and two of the farmers, and he brought them into the yard, coming straight on. They fanned out, covering all the buildings in a show of armed strength that made any thought of fight vanish from the minds of Dannon's men.

"Where is he?" Gunnison asked; he spoke to the foreman.

"He stays in town," the man said. "His missus went in just after midnight last night. With Dal Rainsford. She ain't come back."

"I'm going to ask you once; have you seen Big Sam, Roan Banner, or Deacon?"

The foreman shook his head and he looked at his men and they shook their heads. "What's this all about?" he asked.

"Get your boss to tell you," Gunnison said. He wheeled his horse and led his men out of the yard. When he swung around toward Kyle Burdett's range, Carlyle sided him and shouted over the sound of the horses.

"What makes you think they'd go there?"

"They can't go to town," Gunnison said. "Deacon's hurt. They have to go somewhere."

"I didn't expect to find them at Dannon's."

"I didn't either, but it was worth looking into."

Talk wasn't easy, riding fast, and they said no more. An hour took them across Dannon's range, across his town road; they came on a small herd and pushed through rather than riding around it, then splashed across a creek and entered Burdett's range.

The sun was in their eyes, but rising, an orange flare building an early heat. In Gunnison's mind, Banner and Big Sam were trapped and didn't know it, but many men like them had fallen for the same false sense of security, thinking that there was room to run in open country. But run where? A man had to have a place to go in order to run. They couldn't go to town because Hank Freeman was there and the townspeople were there and they'd know all about it; Banner couldn't go there, couldn't take the train out, couldn't go to the doctor with Deacon. And he wouldn't get far making it to another town.

Deacon would slow them down or he wouldn't last. Or Banner would get tired of being held back and kill Deacon. There wasn't anything the man could do that was right and Gunnison knew it.

They'd have to hole up at Dannon's place, or at Burdett's; there just wasn't any other choice.

Finally they saw Burdett's house and buildings in the distance, tawny and weathered under the bland morning sun, and as they drew near, coming on in a line abreast, running their horses, they saw Deacon in the yard, and Banner there, crouched behind the dead horse.

When they were a hundred yards out, Banner raised his rifle as though to fire at them, then changed his mind and threw it away and stood with his hands high over his head; the taste of death had been strong on his tongue and he had rejected it, for he was not a man who felt that it was a good trade to die as long as you took one of *them* with you. Heroes did this. Patriots did it. But men like Roan Banner could not.

Skillet men swarmed into the yard; they disarmed everyone and Gator went over to the porch and dragged Big Sam over to where Gunnison and the others had dismounted.

The fear in the man gushed up and he tried to break away from Gator and got his nose bloodied for his trouble; he was pushed over to stand by Roan Banner. Skillet riders looked into the outbuildings and remained in the saddle like park policemen, circulating, watching Burdett's men, which they had never really trusted anyway.

Burdett's wife came out, crying, afraid now, and Gunnison said, "Go to her, man."

"I thought I had to stand with them," Burdett said, looking at Big Sam and Roan Banner.

"You think you belong there?" Carlyle asked.

"Not by a damned sight," Burdett said and went to his wife.

Gator came up and said, "There's going to be no trouble here."

Gunnison turned to Simmons and said, "Go on back to your family. Tell Jellico and Ridenhour and the others that I want to see them in town, at the bank, around four this afternoon."

The farmer nodded and turned to his horse. Then he said, "These two, do you mean to hang them?"

"They'll be in jail, if you want to see them."

"I have no wish for that," Simmons said, and stepped into the saddle; he was clumsy on a horse and rode out, beating his feet inelegantly and bouncing in the saddle.

"We're done here," Gunnison said. "Get them mounted, Gator. Find a horse for Banner." He walked over to the porch where Burdett stood with his wife. "You've been no neighbor at all. I want you in town this afternoon. At the bank."

"I've had enough," Burdett said. "I just want out."

"You'll be there," Gunnison said flatly, "or I'll have you brought in."

"Can't you just leave me alone?"

"Why, damn you, Burdett, when did you ever leave Skillet alone? You do as you're told because you're in trouble and I'm not sure yet just how much."

He wheeled and walked to his horse and swung up; the others were waiting and they rode out of Burdett's yard.

Harry Wilson was very cooperative; he normally closed his bank at three-thirty and the meeting at four o'clock did not inconvenience him. Judge Caldwell arrived with Hank Freeman, then Simmons and the other farmers showed up. Carlyle came in, and then Burdett, who seemed nervous.

Gunnison had heard about Dannon's death at the railway station and there was no talk about it. Freeman had questioned Dal Rainsford and the clerk and then sent Cora Dannon home and no one in town thought that she would ever come to trial for it.

Dal Rainsford was the last to show up; he needed a shave

and a night's sleep and the last two days had aged him, sobered him. He sat down and put his hat on the floor and rolled a cigaret, then looked at Charlie Gunnison.

"It's been a year," Gunnison said, "since Old Man Rainsford died and left his will. I've tried to stick to the agreement we made. To some, I may have done so. To others, I've failed. Myself, I believe that I've failed because it was not possible to do otherwise. You'd think that when a man dies, the chance to know him is gone. But that's not so. In spite of his strength, he was weak. And he was afraid he'd live to face the truth about his children. I'm sure he knew how Sam would end. I'm sure he had little hope for Lana." He paused and looked around the room. "But he wanted me to try because he couldn't. Now some will say I didn't do right, didn't try hard enough. I would agree. A man can always look back on a thing and wish he'd done differently." He put a hand to his cheek and scratched his beard stubble. "It may be that what I'm going to do now is wrong, but I think something has to be done. Skillet comes close to ruling this section of Texas. George Dannon's dead; there's no fight left there. Burdett, if you so much as raised an eyebrow, Skillet could ride on you and put you down."

"I know that," Burdett said.

"Fields, there wouldn't be any trouble between your range and mine." He looked at the farmers. "If Skillet decided you were not welcome, you'd go because you wouldn't have any other choice." His glance touched Dal Rainsford. "It's going to take a man to run Skillet and run it right. It's going to take a man with heart to decide what has to be done. What are you going to do, Dal?"

"Me? Do I have to decide?"

"Yes, because I'll be standing at the depot day after tomorrow with my wife, waiting to catch the northbound train," Gunnison said.

Rainsford looked around the room a moment, then stepped on his cigaret. His glance settled on Kyle Burdett. "Because you haven't much spine saved your life, didn't it? You'll never be a neighbor a man can trust. You've got 'til fall to sell your place and clear out."

"You can't make a man do that!" Burdett said.

"Can't I?"

He stared at the man and finally Burdett nodded. "I'll sell."

Dal Rainsford looked at the farmers. "I've never liked farmers, but that's because I never knew any. You knew how cattlemen felt, yet you came to the home place the night of the fire. It could be that this country needs people like that. You want the land you're on, then Skillet will sell it to you. This country's changing. It was bound to happen. Maybe it's a good change. Does that suit you?"

"It's more than fair," Simmons said. "We want to get along."

"You will," Rainsford said. "Don't you think cattlemen would rather live in peace than fight? It costs a lot of money for cattlemen to fight. The range goes to hell and the work goes to pot. The cattle business, like farmin', is a dawn to dark, year 'round job, and then some."

"We're not the only farmers looking for good land," Simmons said. "What of the others who will come?"

"Skillet may sell them land and it may not. It depends on the man."

"There's a matter of Dannon's property," the banker said. "I'm sure his widow would sell it cheaply enough if a man—"

"What the hell's the matter with you? Damn it, ain't there been enough thieves around here to suit you?" He had a genuine, full anger and Harry Wilson retreated a step.

"I was just thinking that as a businessman—"

"My advice is for you to quit thinkin'," Rainsford snapped.

Fields Carlyle chuckled and commented, "Better listen to that, Harry. You're going to be doing business with him a lot of years." He stood up and lit a cigar. "Is there anything I can do for you, Dal? If not, I'll take my men and get on out to my place."

"I appreciate your help," Rainsford said.

Carlyle walked over to Gunnison and shook hands. "I

guess I won't see you again, but it's been my pleasure, Charlie. Something to remember and talk about. A little good and a little bad. Goodbye, Charlie."

"Goodbye," Gunnison said. "If you ever come north—"

"No chance of that," Carlyle said.

He smiled and stepped out and a moment later he rode out of town. Simmons said, "Now there's a nice fellow."

"You'd never think," Freeman said, "that fifteen years ago he was an outlaw and gunfighter, would you?"

Simmons showed his surprise. "Is that so?" He rubbed his hands together aimlessly. "Well, I suppose if there's nothing else—" He got up and stepped to the door and Burdett got up also, and the other farmers.

Judge Caldwell cleared his throat. "There will be papers to be drawn up. In a week, shall we say? You can come to my home when you're in town again."

This satisfied them, a promise from legal authority, and they went out. Dal Rainsford walked to the window and looked out. "Lana's at the hotel, Charlie. What do I say to her? What do I do?"

"Do what you think is right?"

"She hasn't anything now," Dal said. "Nothing at all." He turned around and looked at Gunnison. "Everyone around here knows she took up with George Dannon. If I give her money, it won't last long, will it?" He shook his head. "She'll spend the rest of her life wishing she was in Chicago or some big city, but there isn't any place for her but here." He puffed his cheeks and sighed. "Charlie, if I get in trouble sometime, can I call on you?"

"No," Gunnison said. "I wouldn't come, Dal."

"I guess I see your point. It's no good, fightin' another man's battles, is it?"

"A waste of time," Gunnison admitted.

There was nothing holding Rainsford now, and he had many things to do, few of them really pleasant; he nodded and stepped out and after he closed the door, Judge Erwin Caldwell said, "I think you did what the old man wanted you to do, Charlie. You saved one of his sons." He got up and buttoned his coat. "According to the terms of the agreement between you and Old Man Rainsford, you're to get the profits made during your tenure. It will take a few days, a week, perhaps, for Harry to go over the books and reach a figure. Do you want to wait and—"

"No, let me draw five hundred dollars on it. I want to take my family back to Wyoming."

"All right," Caldwell said. "Where shall I send it?"

"General Delivery, Cheyenne."

"Consider it done," Caldwell said. "Thanks for letting us use the bank, Harry." He put on his hat and stepped to the door; Gunnison opened it and they stepped out onto the walk. "In another year," he said, "Sintown will be dead. Farmers do that, you know. They clean up a place. Their wives don't like gambling and wild women and booze running free. I've seen it happen before. It'll happen here." He peeled a cigar from his leather case and bit off the end. "You ought to stay for the trial, Charlie."

"I know how it'll turn out."

"Well, the only evidence against Sam is his brother's testimony," Judge Caldwell said. "Of course, Banner's guilty; there's no doubt of that."

"I don't care if they turn Sam loose," Gunnison said frankly.

The judge stared. "Why, that's a strange thing to say."

"I only wanted to make sure he'd been caught. Do you see my point?"

"Yes, I believe I do," Caldwell said.

Gunnison walked over and ducked under the hitchrail and untied his horse; he stepped into the saddle. "Goodbye, judge. If you ever get to Wyoming—"

"I won't," Caldwell said.

"And I won't be back."

"Yes, I know. Good luck. My best to your wife."

At the end of the street, Gunnison lifted the horse into a trot and thought that it was good to be leaving, and a little bad too; it was always a mixture, never clear cut one way or another and he had felt this way before, in other towns and other lands, and he supposed that would never change because he always left something of himself in these places and it would be this way until he was used up, with nothing left to give.

But this was the last; he really felt that. In two weeks he'd have over ten thousand dollars in his pocket, and that would buy just the kind of an outfit he wanted, about four thousand acres free and clear, with enough left over to stock it and run it for over a year.

This was his last job. He'd thought that before, but this time he knew it was so; it was a feeling he had, not like before, no elation, so sense of haste to get on with his own life.

He was just through and that was it.

When he arrived at the scarred yard where Skillet's buildings had stood, his wife left the camp by the well and came to meet him; he put his arms around her and kissed her and she said, "Mrs. Simmons gave me some clothes and Mrs. Ridenhour gave me some things for the baby. I've packed them in a bundle." She looked at his face. "We are leaving, aren't we? It's done, isn't it?"

"Yes. Glad?"

"No. Sad perhaps."

"This is my last job," he said.

She didn't ask him if he really meant it or if he was promising; she understood that he meant it and just put her arm around him. They went over to the shade and he picked up the baby and sat down and rocked in on his knees. The sun was hot and he took off his hat and held it over the baby to give it some shade.

Out on the prairie a freak of wind formed up a dust devil, picking up a piece of Texas a grain at a time and whirling it around and aloft. Gunnison watched it and thought of the green flanked mountains of Wyoming.